PAUL SAYER

Paul Sayer was born and brought up in South Milford, near Leeds. His first novel, THE COMFORTS OF MADNESS, published in 1988, won the Constable Trophy for Fiction, the Whitbread First Novel Prize, and the Whitbread Book of the Year Award. It is being translated into seven languages and is available in Sceptre.

He is married, with a young son, and lives in York.

sceptre

Paul Sayer

HOWLING AT THE MOON

To my late mother

First published in Great Britain in 1990 by Constable and Company Ltd.

Sceptre edition 1991

Sceptre is an imprint of Hodder and Stoughton Paperbacks, a division of Hodder and Stoughton Ltd.

British Library C.I.P.

Sayer, Paul
  Howling at the moon.
  I. Title
  823'.914[F]

  ISBN 0-340-53176-2

Printed and bound in Great Britain for Hodder and Stoughton Paperbacks, a division of Hodder and Stoughton Ltd., Mill Road, Dunton Green, Sevenoaks, Kent TN13 2YA. (Editorial Office: 47 Bedford Square, London WC1B 3DP) by Clays Ltd., St Ives plc.

ONE

The day before, Michael Crumly's wife had arrived home with her thick dark hair newly shorn. Where once there had been a fat straggling animal of waves and curls there was now a new shape tamed to Susan's slender neck, brought forward in a misty fringe, with only a vague parting to suggest the way it had been before.

Michael imagined the soft clumps on the hairdresser's floor, his wife's cool smile of approval and her burning amber eyes reflected in the mirror opposite. And he pictured some equally satisfied young man, having performed this service, his hands resting on Susan's shoulders, his work done. These images troubled Michael. He felt his wife should have told him what she was going to do.

'I'm sorry,' Susan said, sensitive to her husband's mute annoyance. 'You don't like it.'

'It makes you look different,' he replied, forcing a smile, looking away. 'I think it suits you. Really . . .' he lied.

'It was something I felt I wanted to do. I thought you might be pleased. It seems I was mistaken,' she said plainly. 'It will grow again, given time.' Then she removed herself to another part of their small terraced house, knowing she could not compete with her husband's silence.

This was so unexpected, Michael thought.

That irritating mite of alarm and disapproval stayed with him for the rest of the evening and was the first thing in his mind when he woke early the next day.

Now his mild exasperation had given way to brooding, to a sombre belief that Susan was a different creature now, changed, animated by that disquieting event of a month before. He tried to reason with himself, feeling he was over-reacting, wishing to dispel his continued sense of having been deceived by Susan, insisting that this was a trifling matter which he should forget all about. Things were bound to be different for them now. But no comfort came from these applied rationalizations.

Through the cleft at the top of the closed green curtains he could see the beginning of another bright September day. From the street outside he heard the sound of car doors slamming like rare drum beats and the wary exchange of monosyllabic greetings between the young professionals who lived here and the older residents – market traders, taxi-drivers, process workers – who formed, yet, the majority of the street's population and who, through their long tenancy, viewed the area proprietorially, scarcely tolerating those wealthy intruders who came, these days, to make their homes there. Children began scampering along the pavement beneath their bedroom window, their feet thudding softly at fluctuating pace.

In the early evening these same youngsters, infants and older children alike – all the offspring of the street's 'original' inhabitants – would congregate outside Mr Ellis-Boyd's off-licence on the corner, peering through the gaps in the blinds that shaded the shop's stock from the sun, tempting the old man's anger with their presence, restlessly tormenting each other. That band of time, between six and eight-thirty, belonged to them and even in the depths of winter they would claim it still, their cries piercing and shrill in the night, emanating from both ends of the street and from its many shadows. Eventually, one by one, they would cede the evening to the adults: aggressive young women in white high heels, rolling-shouldered men in tight-waisted trousers and baggy shirts, all taking to the town in angry pursuit of pleasure. And from any of the one hundred and two houses a dinner-suited young man and his taffeta-gowned partner might also appear, stepping into a waiting cab that might take them to a corporate or theatrical evening in the West End. The old, though, like the frail and the fearing the world over, rarely left their homes after twilight. But each weekday morning, as on this morning, the mood in the street was different – the City workers loaded the paper chattels of their businesses into their cars with brisk, concentrated energy, while the factory hands shambled along with dissension in their voices and resentment and resignation etched in their looks.

Michael Crumly felt tense and dried out. He wondered if he had slept at all. Many hours before, still in the same day to his mind, Susan had once again seemed to want to bridge their recent unvoiced differences by making love. Michael's response had been forced, distantly controlled and unsuccessful. While he had held her, his arms rigid, his fingers knotted, he had felt nothing for her, being still preoccupied with her new appearance, occasionally touching the nape of her neck, tracing the line of her hair with the tip of his finger. He had apologized, reluctantly, not really believing that any apology was due from him. 'You're such a worrier,' Susan had replied, already half-immersed in her dreams, her private world. 'You think too much. That's your trouble. You think too much about everything.'

A milk float whined up the road and Michael lay on his side, facing his wife, knowing he should wake her. Today, he thought, he might deliberately annoy her by making her late on this, only her eighth day back at work. Then he dismissed the idea as wanton, knowing he did not want to heighten the tension that had existed between them for the last month. She turned on to her back, her breasts flat under her Mickey Mouse nightshirt which, coupled with the new hairstyle, made her look disturbingly masculine. He noted the tiny facial tics that accompanied her at the times of her secret dreaming in this the hour of lightest sleep. At close quarters, he examined the soft white line of skin underneath the cap of newly trimmed hair, the occasional wires of grey in the brown, and he felt the same anger – it seemed nothing less – and a fleeting loathing for Susan, an impulsive distaste of which he was consciously quite ashamed.

Eventually, sternly reminding himself that it was his duty, he nudged her gently with his elbow, calling her name twice. She nodded, forcing her eyes wide open a few seconds later. Then she rose and drowsily began picking up clothing from about the bedroom. Michael turned his back to her, glimpsing her only as she passed to cross the landing to the bathroom. Then he heard her hurry down the stairs, her tread quick and light, and into the kitchen where she chinked crockery and opened drawers and cupboard doors.

A few minutes later he got out of bed himself, covering his nakedness with his tattered yellow dressing-gown, lingering a little longer, willing the time to advance further so that he might have to confront his wife only briefly before she had to go. At last, he went down to the small lounge next to the kitchen, sitting in one corner of the beige corduroy-upholstered chesterfield that filled almost half of one side of the room.

Susan was already dressed in a cream pleated blouse and a plain brown skirt. Now she need only shuffle her feet into her flat suede shoes and pick her coat from the peg in the hall for her to be ready to go to work.

'Tea?' she asked.

'You don't have time,' said Michael. 'I'll get it myself.'

'It's no bother. I've already poured. It's the new rose-flavoured stuff. You'll have to try it.'

She produced a steaming red mug for him from the kitchen. She must have been listening for me rising, he thought. How he hated being anticipated in his movements, even in this small way. He took the mug and set it down on the low plastic cube table beside the sofa.

This morning Susan seemed more active and buoyant than usual: her work persona, Michael thought, irritated further by her light, bustling presence. She paused momentarily in her fluttering routine, smiling blankly at him. He pretended to be visually absorbed by some detail in the storage heater by the door, knowing that Susan was trying to seduce him into conversation.

'Grumpy today?' she asked.

'I'm all right.'

She sat down on the edge of the armchair, sipping tea.

In the early days of their five-year marriage they had always scrupulously insisted on discussing every point of conflict in their relationship – their failure to please each other in bed the previous night would certainly have meant that this morning they would have risen together, perhaps half an hour early, to talk the matter through, insistent that they achieved some explanation of the situation. And they would have sought a remedy at the earliest possible opportunity. But nowadays Michael tended only to want to ignore such matters. Indeed, in the face of the most exacting problem in their marriage – which they had recently endured – they had hardly chosen to consult with each other beyond simply establishing their individual points of view which, in essence at least, had mercifully concurred.

'Not going to work today?' Susan asked.

'One of the advantages of being self-employed is that you work when it pleases you. I have no fixed times, no one telling me where I should be . . .' He checked himself, knowing this emphatic kind of talk was uncalled-for. 'Yes. I am going to work today.'

'Only asking,' said Susan, blowing on her drink, staring at the blank television screen in the corner. 'You look a bit under the weather, that's all. You're not ill again, are you?'

'I feel fine,' said Michael, an impatient sigh mingled with his words. He stifled the impulse to snap at her, holding it in his chest as she stood and went through to the kitchen before brushing past him on her way back to slip on the shoes she had placed earlier by the cold fire.

'I'll see you this evening, then,' she said.

'Yes. Of course.'

'And you will eat some lunch today, won't you? It does you no good to go without.'

'Yes, I will eat lunch. I'll get something from the baker's.'

In the moment they used to reserve for a farewell embrace he could only offer a flinty smile which Susan returned, squeezing his arm before passing through to the hall and closing the front door softly behind her.

Michael shuffled his bare feet on the swirl-textured blue carpet. Alone now, he felt uncomfortable with the silence that remained, guilty about this solitude he had wished for himself and about the vacuum their inarticulacy was creating between them.

TWO

By nine-forty the confluence of hurrying bodies heading for trains and buses had thinned and Michael walked to his studio in hot sunlight. He rather liked this time, feeling a sense of superiority over those who must work according to predestined hours. He passed along two avenues, down a fenced snicket and into the High Street. A smell of pastry and warm meat wafted from a baker's shop, making his stomach roll. He never ate breakfast and his appetite had been generally poor for a long time, making him thinner than he could ever recall having been before. In the newsagent's store beneath his studio he bought a packet of chewing gum and the *Independent* and, on leaving, he turned sharply left to unlock the door which opened on to the staircase leading to his rooms.

Michael Crumly was a graphic designer, if anyone asked him, though he was always at a loss to explain the precise nature of his occupation. Here, in this place, he worked alone, managing all the aspects of a small business in addition to the artwork commissions he received. He was a methodical, conscientious designer – Slow Michael, he would often whisper, trying, usually unsuccessfully, to chide himself into working more quickly, perhaps to meet an unreasonable deadline: Dozy Michael, Michael the Sloth, get on, get on. But the work suited him, by and large, and he had fared well over the eleven years that he had been there. In his youth he had wanted to paint 'creatively', 'expressively', but he quickly realized the mediocrity of his experimental efforts, the imitation in his work, and, more importantly, he came to understand that the world spent little on 'genuine' art. At twenty he quit his course at Leeds Art School to go south in search of work, eventually finding a job with a large 'design agency'. Here, at the firm of Porritt & Porritt, he learned to suppress his artistic whims, taming the urge, aping the craftsmanship of his new, seasoned colleagues, anxious to please, listening to every scrap of grudgingly offered advice, taking slight criticisms too much to heart. He had to deal directly with the agency's clients, learning quickly, nervously, how to anticipate their often deficient, sometimes grandiose visions of the way their products should be sold: 'Tell them they need me. Me. You must make the world believe that life is impure without my matches/shoes/paint/lawnmowers/lager/book/shirts/air freshener/peace of mind. Tell them how they must want these things. Sell for me. Sell me!'

The days were long and trying, and more than once Michael felt appalled by the commercialism that seemed to dominate everything in this world he had discovered. Soon, though, he was able to control his output, to distance himself from the base purpose of the signs he painted, the toy boxes he designed. He found a splendid satisfaction in the growth of an image for, say, a billboard poster for a new make of beer, or a supermarket logo, and he derived an almost sensual pleasure from the developing craft with which he was able to bring a 'message' to a simple and direct life. Indeed, a finished design might be a matter for surreptitious gloating on his part, long glances stolen when his blasé colleagues were distracted elsewhere, views he might seek from the side, from close up, as he departed from the room, though he rarely bothered to see where the thing was to be displayed, feeling a sad sense of decay, of ephemerality, in a sign hoisted maybe fifty feet high among the elements. Steadiness and surety of hand, an eye for impact, balance, subtlety of colour and shade, the readiness with which he was able to adapt to modern trends, the way in which he learned to recycle ideas time and time over – all these acquired skills led him to believe that there might be no more than a handful of principles to graphic design, and he imagined, one day, that he might clarify them in a handbook. But this vision became lost over the seven years of low pay and automatic response that he spent with Porritt & Porritt.

For a long time the trappings of his job had preoccupied him in a way he found difficult to define. The labyrinthine working structure of the company perplexed him and he could never properly fathom its intricacy, the way it functioned as a whole, its means of survival. And he worried, irrationally, about the claustrophobic corridors, the way he felt the firm had absorbed him, his never properly outlined standing in this ungainly giant.

I have been sleeping for too long, he thought, one morning on the two-mile walk from his flat to the agency. I have forgotten myself, lost my sense of living, he believed as he stopped in the middle of a High Street, looking up at a hand-scrawled 'To Let' notice sellotaped behind two dusty casement windows (two panes cracked, one smashed through) above a cluttered newsagent's shop. He sat on a bench opposite, drawn and enchanted by the two windows, their flaking paint and crumbling sills, the light and vague shapes cast by the early morning sun on the bleak yellow interior. In such a place I might survive, he thought, become myself, exist on my own terms. My sleepwalking has brought me here.

His heart was heavy in his chest, his head spinning

with tumultuous suggestions. By mid-afternoon, knowing he must act without hesitation, feeling the power and purity of this impulse, he had signed the lease and tendered his resignation by telephone to an indifferent secretary.

His landlord, Mr Wallender, the newsagent, a young, active, happy man, gave him two old tables and a chair. With his small savings he was able to buy cheap, basic tools, the minimum requirements to start himself off. Slowly, uneasily, with some courage, he overcame his shyness and acquired a small list of regular clients, including several disaffected former customers of Porritt & Porritt. But he never really grew to like this side of things, resenting the increased personal contact that was necessary now he was on his own. He shunned familiarity with his clients, and was sometimes over-zealous in his pursuit of outstanding accounts, imagining all kinds of duplicity, threatening legal action in the first instance when he should have reserved that as a last resort. But he did learn to cherish his independence, here, in this one square room, this unhoney-combed place where he need not be hurried and where, if a prospective client rang whose voice he did not care for, he need only tell the man that he had the wrong number or that the business no longer existed!

For a brief time his early rapture with his work was rekindled and he even thought of resurrecting his old art-school ambitions of 'serious' painting, but the necessity of earning a living was uppermost in his mind and he distanced himself from that old longing, even tiring, eventually, of congratulating himself on his truly polished designs, turning quickly away from a sweet-box 'rough' or an estate agent's sign, his only wish being that the thing might dry quickly enough for him to cover it and have it on its way. Instead, he found a new and unexpected diversion, a facet of his business life that satisfied his instinct for playfulness and harmony: accountancy.

How he began to adore those clean, well-ordered columns of figures. What stories they told! In his dark-green tall ledgers he could divine movement, a new concept of design, a history of work from the one-third deposit taken at the start of a commission to the final embracing conclusion of the balance paid. He loved the way figures could complement each other, the way he had to apply his mind to seek a mortally necessary balance, and he would be in private rapture when he contemplated his expenses accounts and the ways in which he manipulated them. The savings he could make on electricity, on the type of paper he bought, the paints! Ah, the hard, unsentimental truth of numbers – gross profits, net profits, forecasts, balance sheets, depreciating assets (the mystery and magic of these – he possessed so many serviceable items that the books deemed no longer in existence!). He discovered an aptitude for arithmetic and scorned the idea of buying a calculator. He compiled his accounts in drafts, each in pencil, until the final item was prepared, in ink, in his finest hand. Yet he was not a parsimonious man – he felt genuinely uncomfortable with the idea that others might see him motivated only by self-interest: there was more to it than that, so much more . . . Rather he insisted only that the machinery of his accountancy worked with unerring efficiency, its actual results (in his best year, 1987, he made more than £32,000) giving him little concern, the profits being channelled out of his working life, away from the field of his occupation to his one personal bank account, or to his building society, from which he accepted a very poor rate of interest.

This year, business had been slow and he felt himself becoming slovenly, unable to concentrate on any aspect of his work, not even his beloved accounts. His one lucrative commission had been for the cover of a 'Greatest Hits' album by a long-ago disbanded rock band of whose genuinely successful singles most people would only be able to name one: that small classic 'Moral Graffiti (In My Heart)'. Before him, on this morning, was a seven-by-four-foot painting, oils on heavily sized cheap chipboard that would warp if not quickly and securely hung, of a gently undulating snowfield beneath a bright blue sky that was speckled with small white clouds underscored in grey. The snowfield was dissected by an arc of footprints that led from a distant, off-centre, empty red car, the four doors of which were mysteriously open. The effect was of garish conception, brash, shallow, one of four 'originals' copied from an old calendar supplied by Michael's client, a middle-aged, excitable businessman called De Lacy. They were all for the Acidscape discothèque he was opening in town. He had always worried Michael, right from the moment he had shaken the ragged-edged calendar under the designer's nose, saying, 'I like the ideas here very much. There is a message here, yes? Many messages. I want these paintings very, very bright. Their theme must go in here (forefinger jabbing inches from Michael's pupil), and register here (palm tapping the back of Michael's head), and be felt . . . here (fist on sternum)!' Then he laughed. Michael had thought, in advance, that he might have trouble exacting the balance due for this work.

Dutifully, though, this morning, he picked up his brushes from the draining board next to the old white sink and began deepening the midnight blue tint at the top of the painting to heighten the contrast between the sky and the ice-white of the lower half of the picture. Dull work.

Thus the hours passed, the only sounds being the low rumble of traffic in the High Street, Michael's feet shuffling on the dusty floor, the whispered touches of his brush-strokes and the jangling of Mr Wallender's shop doorbell, muffled, as if a great distance away, and the only movement being the red roof of an occasional double-decker bus sliding along the windowsill.

He paused only once from his somnambulent routine, at twelve-thirty, to make coffee. By mid-afternoon he felt very weary, the muscles in his chest and shoulders ached, and his stomach felt sore and squeezed. He still could not bear the thought of food. With an heroic effort he applied the last flourishes to what he knew to be a desultory piece of work, though it would be good enough to satisfy the owner of the new Acidscape discothèque. At last he turned away from the painting and washed his brushes with meanly gauged drops of spirit from the big red plastic bottle under the sink. Then he sat at his desk near the door, interlacing his fingers and stretching them until they clicked. He yawned and stared idly at the clutter of his studio: inks, paints, tweezers, rubber cement, a T-square leaning against the wall, books and papers on the worktops under the windows, old drawings tumbling from the shelves of an open cupboard. He rubbed his eyes and breathed deeply, saying aloud, 'I am losing my grip. Lazy Michael.'

He opened his accounts file, the input ledger in which he intended to log some trifling item of stationery for which he had the receipt in his jacket pocket, where he found a postcard-sized pencil drawing of a face. It was a lateral impression, quickly, stylishly done, with only four sure but faint lines to represent eye and mouth. Indeed, there was little of the turned-away face that could be seen for the mass of the image was made up of hair, tangled, tumbling: Susan's hair. For one short second he was amused that he could not remember having drawn this picture – and he truly had no recollection of it, nor could he think of any motive for its creation – then he succumbed to a dull sense of depression, a reawakening to the new differences that existed between him and his wife, the mute distinctions that his work that day had allowed him to forget, if only for a while. Now his antagonism towards her returned, more precisely felt, his dislike of the way he fancied she was changing when he was not, of the way she had cut her hair without telling him, of the secret thoughts in her mind that she was not sharing with him, and he was moved to a quiet despair when he thought again of the scene between them both – which he saw as being the start of all this – just over a month ago . . .

THREE

Given now to endless mental reconstructions of recent history, Michael remembered how he had found something faintly absurd and profitless in sitting in a small café, so close to home, on that Sunday afternoon four weeks and four days before. If they had wanted to eat they need not have left the house. Then he had counselled himself, thinking that this petty reflection was part of his woodenness, born of the poverty of his imagination. He would never have been able to suggest, or derive pleasure from, such a trifling activity as this, which had been Susan's idea.

She had looked roseate that August day, self-absorbed and yet cheerful in the bright red and green of that place which filled with bodies seeking shelter from the rain, cramming behind formica-topped tables: a press of walkers, local-history seekers, road-repairers idling on double-time, listless children who glared at each other while their mothers smoked and exchanged plaintive conversation. Michael mused vaguely about the fragments of all their lives being wasted in that garish room; the way they all, himself included, seemed to have opted for giving the impression of being only half-alive, a very British public trait.

Susan had seemed to feast on all this, scooping tiny crescents of gâteau on to the tip of her spoon, her big eyes drawn by each moving man, woman and child. Michael envied her nimble spirit, her susceptibility to the most inconsequential diversion or charm. He wondered if she might sometimes be annoyed with his poor sense of levity, his undemonstrative attitude to so much of life, his deification of only the most basic requirements for survival. She caught him staring at her and offered a half-moon smile between mouthfuls of chocolate icing. Talk to her. Say something, damn you.

'Nice cake?'

'Cream's souring.'

In a shape of time, a displaced time, removed from this, everything had seemed so new, so appropriate. That other world of six years before, when they had first met. He was thirty-one, then, and Susan just twenty-five. In his mind's eye, the memory he did not trust very much, he thought of her as being more reflective, more judgemental than now, and in appearance more angular, not as attractive as she was today. They had married within fourteen weeks, he for the second time, his first marriage having been a brief and unfortunate affair. For two years they had loved hard and unflinchingly, seeking each other with a will, but it could not have gone on like that, he could not have borne such intensity forever. Sometimes, though, he looked back and regretted the caution he had imposed – he always assumed it was of his devising – on their relationship, shrinking, it seemed to him, from the powerful intimacy that threatened to overwhelm them both. Could a whole lifetime have been spent that way? He did not know. Instinctively now, almost purposefully, they had begun to establish their differences from each other. Michael had often voiced a suspicion he held about Susan's practicality and the ease with which she seemed to accept and face a preposterous, deceitful world. Susan timidly declared her fear of his 'brooding intelligence', though when he challenged her she could not really define this.

At first it was as if, by declaring that which they

found objectionable or threatening in each other, these aspects of themselves might disappear. This was naïvety itself, Michael thought; a watery psychological whim of the times – open the wound and let it heal. Nonsense. Nowadays they rarely argued, knowing the value of peace, the futility of their disputes which existed nonetheless, yet the causes of which each suppressed until they could not hold them any longer and their anger surfaced, in cycles of a few months at a time. This ire was dimly focused, tangential, only weakly rooted in the truth of their dissatisfaction with each other.

They knew no real hardship. 'If we were to be honest,' Michael would insist, 'I would say that we invent our problems. We have money, much more than we need . . .'

'Is money central to a marriage?' Susan would counter.

'It is in some, I'm sure.'

'It's not as important as you think. It's never as important as people think. Money's a pastime, a very pleasurable distraction.'

Michael would agree, adding, 'That aside then, I do not believe we are unhappy. I don't think either of us has the capacity for unhappiness.'

Susan might then say, 'Perhaps we should make more space, allow ourselves more freedom from each other?'

This same conversation took many forms and Michael would nod in tacit concurrence with the last principle, though it might privately worry him and, if he pursued the matter, neither seemed capable of describing 'freedom' nor of stating how they might take up this 'option'.

Of their few friends in London, most had children now and they saw them only infrequently, feeling often that they were intruding on their time-sapped lives, bringing with them the unwanted taint of an existence that their friends had forgone and which more than one modern couple admitted they envied Michael and Susan for hanging on to. Childless then, by fierce agreement, much of their energy in the early years went into the ornamentation of their house – well-chosen, expensive carpets, the chesterfield, a chiming clock in the front lounge. Susan, to Michael's concealed rancour, would call the place their 'cottage', and he would counter the cosiness of this epithet and all that it might imply about his wife, perhaps after too much wine in the evening, by referring to the 'tyrannized, unforgivably misled' railway and munitions workers for whom the houses had been built in the first decade of the century. Into such conversations he would repetitively haul maudlin details about his working-class upbringing, boring Susan – the only daughter of a wealthy Midlands businessman – enormously, though she would smile, feigning interest, gracefully tolerating his many barbed remarks about her middle-class background, tiring when his drunkenness, which was rare, brought obtuse pronunciations about London; 'this miserable place . . .'

Within two years they had gravitated from an early intoxication with each other back towards themselves, retreating into small corners of their private imaginations. Yet still they accepted each other with an unbegrudged respect, creating a small civilization, a silently prescribed dependence, friendship, sometimes more . . .

Once, not long ago, Michael contracted a mild form of hepatitis. He was frail in recuperation and Susan cared well for him, showing a strength he had not believed she possessed, a new, different tenderness, sleeping close, cradling his weakness, saying, once: 'I think you are beautiful this way, more beautiful than anyone I have ever known . . .'

But such delicacy was rare these days.

Lately Susan had been guardedly mentioning a move within the financial company for which she worked. She had begun speaking of 'fulfilment' and 'stretching' herself. She also scanned the jobs columns in the papers. Michael, in his usual static, ruminative way, wondered what inferences he might draw from her message of dissatisfaction with life and he would retreat into his impenetrable silence if ever he felt the subject of change was near. Secretly he perhaps feared, above all, the moment when Susan might state that she was not including him in her plans.

'Are you wanting to go home?' she asked. 'You look rather bored.'

'Do I? I'm sorry,' Michael replied. 'Actually I'm rather enjoying it. We should go out more. There's nothing to stop us. We should make the effort.'

'We're becoming lazy, I agree.'

'One night this week, then. I'll try and think of somewhere,' Michael said, knowing he would conveniently forget this suggestion.

Susan sprinkled crumbs from the table to her plate which a flustered-looking young waitress took from her. 'Actually,' she said, 'I'd rather like to go now.'

A new bright sun had lifted a delicious mist from the pavement and Michael breathed deeply, stuffing his hands into the pockets of his heavy coat. Susan slipped her hand around his arm and leaned heavily on him. 'It's funny,' she said.

'What is?'

'Here we are like a couple of old dodderers. Every day we seem to become more like the people we always said we would never be. Don't you think?'

'I'm not sure what you mean,' Michael replied, sensing a pending state-of-the-relationship discussion he would avoid if he could. 'Some things are inevitable –

growing older, more familiar with each other, pacing ourselves for a long life together.'

'I used to think,' Susan reflected, 'that my life would travel spirally, ever upwards, to some plateau of sage-liness, to a knowing, a certainty about who I was, where I was going. Each turn of the spiral would bring me closer to a sacred path, an insight, justification and acceptance of everything.'

'And isn't it that way?'

'When I passed thirty it all seemed to go flat. Death, one day, became a possibility for the first time. I began to see everything going in circles. Repetition, that's all there seems to be. Can you understand that?'

Michael had sensed all this was leading to something. He did not want to talk like this. He never wanted to talk these days. 'We could go back through the Museum Park,' he said, by way of reply.

'That would be nice. I would like that very much,' Susan said, an earnestness in her voice that seemed too passionate a way to respond to such a simple suggestion.

They had walked under the wrought-iron arch in silence, Michael keen to avoid his wife's eyes, looking ahead and up at the straying white clouds stretched and torn over the ugly backs of tall terraced houses and the tower blocks beyond. Pink-faced children were riding their bicycles at breakneck speed along the narrow paved edge of the pond with no apparent sense of fear or jeopardy. Away, somewhere to the west, church bells wrought their solemn, accusing tunes on the air – a noise that always depressed Michael. At Susan's bidding they had sat down on a damp bench. Opposite, an old couple leaned, half-crouched on a low wall. The man was tall, his face crimson, capped with a blitz of white hair. The woman held on to him, deep in her thick coat, her water-filled ankles bursting out of her laced shoes. Michael stared at her face, the fine lines in her cheeks like the channels in delta mud, here and there a calyx of pinched capillaries. Such are the faces of the old, he thought. And the bodies of the old are brittle-limbed, thin-blooded, hard to heal and slow to escape pain. I shall not like being old, he thought, his hand deep in his pocket, tugging at a line of straying cotton which he twined tightly round the tip of his finger.

'Michael?'

He had almost forgotten Susan was there. Her hand was heavy on his arm. He turned to see her sugar-white face. 'Is something the matter?'

'I have to tell you something.'

'What do you have to tell me?' he asked, gently.

She had let go of his arm, clasping her hands in front of her as if in benediction, her eyes half-closed.

'I'm pregnant.'

FOUR

Three weeks later Susan Crumly stared up from her bed at the limp top corner of a rhomboid-patterned, much-laundered orange curtain. The next bed, at the other side of this flimsy screen, was empty. She was dry-eyed, far from tired, and she had the vague sensation of trespassing in someone else's dream. The aluminium-rimmed clock on the wall clicked every fifteen seconds. If she concentrated on this sound the ticks began to seem irregular. She decided to ignore them, rationing herself to glimpses stolen only when she could not bear to look away any longer. Time, in this hard, unsentimental place, was in hiatus, independent of the world without, careless of that place's organization, the order it imposed on time, dividing the chaos up into manageable pieces: days, hours, minutes. How many people must have died here? Susan Crumly wondered. How many last breaths hushed from coarsened mouths, warm corpses grieved over by weeping loved ones, spirits old and young slipping from time, left high and dry, broken, unmade by time, that spiteful, immortal god?

She listened to the low moans of other patients, the soothing hum of a machine she could not begin to understand which fed a mattress behind another filmy curtain, the tubes like black snakes in the pool of light that spread from beneath the ragged hem. There was a reassuring smell of cleanliness, of neutrality deliberately achieved, she thought, wondering, after a while, if the pungent odour might be coming from her own body.

First she had felt a slovenly guilt which she had easily outwitted (that would return, though – God knows how many times in the years that lay ahead) to replace it with a warm, grim sense of purpose, ready acknowledgement of a selfishness which she refused, in her own mind, to label as anything else – not unreadiness, not a strident declaration of female individuality, not an insistence on 'personal freedom', whatever that might be. Now that the 'act' was 'done', there was only a numbness, an elusive sense of liberation (about which she would feel more guilt – damned guilt – is there such a thing as life without it?) and a weak suspension above all these inventions of the neurotic mind. Perhaps, if time might be merciful for once, all this might simply become a dry memory, no more than a factual event in the life of Susan Crumly *née* Thorpe, needing no further analysis or subjective contemplation.

'Will you keep it?' had been Michael's cautious response that day in the park. A little fury had possessed her at that moment of her confession, that instant of admission that had kept her in a cocoon of worry and brainstorming fears for three days. She had wanted to strike out at Michael for his economy of expression. *'No,'* she had replied, steeling herself, realizing she might have expected no more from her taciturn husband, *'I think not.'* She had brought him pain, though, and for a single moment she was pleased, taking a small, perverse satisfaction from seeing him retract into his silence, returning to that zealous guarded world of his own with this shattering information. In the past there had been so many times when she had felt grateful for Michael's reticence, the slowness to reaction that made their life together peaceful,

29

uncluttered with the hysteria and conventions that she felt dominated the existences of so many couples like them. But this once, this one time, vainly, she had hoped for more. 'Will you keep it?' had revealed an intrinsic weakness in Michael that she wished might not be there, an absence of an ultimate reliability she had always had faith in, a dumb maleness that repulsed her. 'Will you keep it?' hived all the responsibility, all the blame, on to her. And had she not sustained this idea by offering dates, excuses, sorrow for her simple forget-fulness (bad luck, that was all, she thought in rare, oh heavens how rare, moments of self-confidence)? 'Will you keep it?' had been a condemnation of her body as a troublesome thing, a bitter response to her physical self, cruel beyond belief. Her body, in those moments, had become a vessel of doom that threatened them both, their lives together, their freedom from each other and, yes, if she thought about it, she looked at it the same way. This prison that is me, she thought, sensing an early lifting of the numbness, her eyes prickling in the poor heavy light, the mumbling and solitude that filled these dark hours on the hospital ward.

This simply will not do, she told herself, seeking consoling thoughts.

Perhaps her parents might have been more under-standing – her father would certainly have paid for a private place. How minute a thing it might have become if she had only gone straight to them. But she knew she did not have the fortitude for presenting them with her dilemma. Indeed, might not her father, perhaps pass-ing from a boardroom meeting to a tryst with an illicit lover, have simply paused in the car-park outside one of his factories, also to tender that heinous question, 'Will you keep it?' Susan had imagined that scene keenly, knowing her father too well, quite unable to conjure up any other fantasy about the way he might react. And her mother? Well, perhaps more laconically inclined:

'What a to-do! How unfortunate. Have you had supper? Work getting you down too, is it?'

Children. What did Susan know about them? Sometimes she had looked after a friend's nine-month-old baby. She had held her, a quiet and good thing, and rocked her to sleep. She had watched over her in the cot, strangely troubled by her fragility and innocence. Susan could never have lived with such delicacy – a feeling that haunted her, making her wonder whether, if she ever had a child of her own, she might not become one of those small-paragraph cases, the mother driven, or through aberration, who dashes at her child. She simply did not like children, she would say, knowing that she really rather feared and envied them.

A dirty light was burgeoning behind the window blinds. Susan glowered at the unglazed Manets and Corots on the shiny buff walls. Now her self-pity was dissipating into something approaching a healthy anger, reproach for those who seemed to wish to occlude her from self-expression, from womanhood, her right to be adult, those who had always kept her from being herself, one way or another – her parents, the teachers at her schools, friends, employers, Michael, her own self. In a few hours she would be able to go home. And with what vengeance would she begin the process of forgetting.

There were nine other 'patients' (she could not now think of herself as being in this category) in this room, most of whom, if not all, must have come for the same reason as her, though she had hardly spoken to those few who had congregated in the dreary lounge at the end of the ward to watch television – *Miami Vice*, *Prisoner: Cell Block H* – before turning in, feigning tiredness, every one of them. Who cares anyway, she thought, clenching her fists beneath the single blue sheet that covered her. Life is too bloody short to worry about other people. Damn it all. Damn everyone.

'First time, dearie?' came a catarrhal voice from the bed opposite. Susan looked at the tiny head above the thick yellow blankets. She had not realized there was anyone there.

'What did you say?' she whispered.

'Don't worry about a thing, my love. You soon get over it. Marvellous they can do it, really. Should be compulsory in some countries, don't you think?'

She had short black hair, weathered skin, gypsy features. She must be fifty years old, Susan thought. Suddenly, loudly and unselfconsciously, the coarse voice filled the ward: 'Get me to the toilet, please.' The woman propped herself up on her elbow and repeated the demand, looking at the floor, awaiting a reply.

Then the nurse appeared, heavy and bustling. 'Shush. You're not to shout like that. You'll wake all the other ladies. And you can't go to the toilet. You know what the doctor said. Stay quiet now and I'll fetch a bedpan.'

'I can't use one of them things. I can't get on it properly. I use the toilet in my own home, so why can't I use it here?' the woman insisted with what seemed to Susan a reasonable argument. 'I have to go,' she went on. 'Now. Me waters are coming away from me.'

'I'll bring the commode then. Just be patient. I'll be back in a minute,' the nurse said, gliding away, twitching curtains as she passed, little bones clicking in her feet.

The woman looked across at Susan and smiled kindly, revealing a few tombstone teeth. 'You look pale, love. Bet you haven't slept. There's many that don't, first time. Feel guilty, they do. But you shouldn't take on about any of this. It's a woman's right. Been here five times before, myself. You soon forget about it, believe me.'

'That's very reassuring,' Susan whispered brightly.

'Why, you'll be away in the morning and out on the town with your boyfriend tonight!'

'Maybe.'

'Course you will. Mark my words. And make sure he pays for it all – it's all his fault, isn't it? No such luck for me though. My bugger's slung his hook back to Norway. Shan't see him again.'

'Oh, I'm sorry.'

'I'm not. Not really . . .' she paused, looking as if she wanted to say more. Then she threw her blankets back, yelling, 'Nurse? Nurse? Oh, I've had all I can take from this place. I'll soon show her.'

'What do you mean?' asked Susan, sitting forward in the bottom half of her own bed. 'What will you do?'

'Wait a minute.' The woman winced as if she had lemon on her tongue. 'There. That's it!'

'That's what?' asked Susan, bright, alive, smiling.

'Pissed the bed, haven't I?' the woman said, her eyes shrinking to pinpricks above the cavernous smile.

Susan bit a handful of her sheet to stifle her unbidden delight.

FIVE

Michael turned the small grey impression around in his paint-discoloured fingers, stroking a corner with his blue thumb. How could he simply *forget* having made this sketch? Once Susan had asked him to paint a portrait of her, and he had seriously intended to do so, though something always worried him about the idea. He had wondered about her presence here, in his studio, the only place he could wilfully complete artistic work of any kind. He had imagined the light formality they would have to adopt while she sat and he examined each minute detail of her. Did he fear the intimacy of the project? Had he been concerned with the kind of interpretation he might make in a portrait? How might his true feelings about her have surfaced in such a coalition of pinks, ochres, yellows, a purple-based brown for the hair? And how, indeed, might she react to such a picture, tinged with his own mind's-eye view of her? He felt she did not really know much about the creative process, the powers and darknesses it could liberate. At first, he had been intrigued by the whole idea, but he found himself prevaricating until she no longer seemed interested in the scheme.

He set the drawing down squarely on the centre of his desk. In what fragment of time in the last few days, weeks, had he turned from his tedious working rituals to bring a pencil, with such obvious thought and deliberation, across this piece of paper?

Once again he was thinking about the conscious control he seemed to be losing over the small actions in his daily existence. Had he not, two days before, *forgotten* to deliver a small rough of a poster which the curator of a museum – a nervy, serious young man whom Michael had felt threatened by on their one, brief meeting – had requested for an exhibition of old telegraphic paraphernalia? He had drawn the thing and felt it was competent, but his 'oversight' had lost him the commission. That was not like him – he had never before succumbed to his customary apprehensions about any of his new clients – for that was surely the reason for his, perhaps subconscious, decision to avoid the work being offered, the contact he would have to renew with someone he simply did not like.

Lately he had felt a recurring, unattached sting of excitement in his blood, in his hands, his head, an odd rush of anticipation, a hint of mania, as if he was on the brink of either a great wisdom or some fearful catastrophe. In his superficial yet most private thoughts, those from the woolly tangle at the front of his mind, he linked this peculiar sensation with Susan, blaming her for the trouble she had brought them, while still knowing that such thoughts were ungenerous. This feeling, in essence, seemed shot through with a certainty he could not understand, a sense of fate, a movement towards an unknown destiny which he could not resist. My head will go 'pop' one of these days, he thought, smiling to himself, sliding the little drawing into the end leaf of his file. '*Pop!*' he shouted as he closed the dark green cover on the columns of figures for which he had no appetite that day. 'Pop, pop, pop, pop,' he recited as he took his jacket from the hook behind the door and skipped down the staircase out into the heaving rush-hour street and the gold-metal sunlight that had not abated all day.

He felt inexplicably light-hearted, aloof from the cares

of his life and work. Turning into the last avenue before their street he thought he might even run the last few hundred yards to the front door. But he did not. Instead he simply breathed and exhaled deeply, straightened his frame, quickened his pace and took care not to smile at the many weary-looking people he passed.

SIX

On a cool September Tuesday, in her lunch-hour, six days after her abortion, Susan Crumly had strolled alone among Oxford Street shoppers, dealers, profferers of free magazines, BBC secretaries, the anonymous titled, and felt she wanted to pray. It was the wanting that was important, she thought.

She had not prayed since childhood, that time she remembered when she would list all her hopes for everyone she knew, thinking of the good she might wish into their lives. For her parents there must be love for each other (of the eternal variety). For her best friend, Sheila Meeney, there should be an early marriage to a handsome Frenchman who must also be wealthy so that she might put to rights her father's failing fortunes which were threatening to take her from the school. For Rowena Geddis, who was ailing, there had to be health and a long life made even happier by helping others less fortunate than her. And a long life too for Susan's Siamese, Estella. For all the world there must be peace to the end of time with no famines, no wars, no natural disasters to bring any more of those awful pictures to the television screen. All these things the nine-year-old Susan elaborately catalogued in her mind before she slept, just in case – one never knew – an angel came and woke her in the night to grant her a single wish. She was always careful never to include any personal requirements in this list. What a smug little darling I was! Susan now thought. How I feared that superstition – which persists to this hour – that someone, somewhere, was making note of all this, ready for the Day of Judgement when all malevolence and charitable acts were weighed against each other. This old, silly idea, the crucible of her guilt, confounded her even now on this day in her thirty-second year as she stumbled over the doorway into Next with the preconceived idea that she might buy some trinket, a small gift to herself to signify that her life might start anew. She paused before a perfume counter, felt nauseated by the sickly smell that caught in her throat, and returned to the street by the second open door.

She had only ever thought of God as a necessary panacea, a compromise for the searching mind's inability to embrace the notion of eternity, its wish not to recognize that this might be all there is, this here and now. Yet to consider the latter, she believed, was the first step on the road to madness. If she were looking for something herself, she decided, it was faith alone; there were no solutions about the after-life to be had. This, she thought, looking at the leaden-shaded, frowning buildings, the human flesh cradled in metal cars pressed manically together, the tarmac welded to pavement to stone to sky, this cannot be everything.

Then she thought of Michael.

My heart must be made of concrete if I cannot accommodate him now. How easily I have forgotten his fear of spontaneity, his rank dread of not being in control. How all this must have hurt him, be hurting him, perhaps at this very minute when he will be closeted away in his studio, alone, ever alone, with only her company to look forward to, only her presence actually wanted in his life. And this thing, this event, had come between them, eroding their old true optimism about the contentment they might achieve in their lives together. It was like night about them. And how she felt she had cherished this emptiness that was now inside her, holding it to herself, using it as an excuse for self-indulgence, seeking sentiment. She must love Michael again, look outwards, get this piece of time out of her memory, desensitize herself to it, exorcize it – what future was there in seeking an oblivion of self-pity?

She was wandering in side-streets now, able to hear the dull even tread of her own feet on the sloping pavement, feeling a heaviness in her calves, a cool breeze at her back that brought the smells of food and exhaust fumes from somewhere else. Across the road she saw a scattering of glass crystals from the shattered window of a parked car. Crates of rubbish were piled in the gutter awaiting collection. She turned into a dark narrow road and unable to walk any further, devoid of will and spirit, she sat down on the steps of a boarded-up chapel and wept, for herself, for Michael, for the child she had not allowed to grow inside her, for all the evil she insisted she must have wrought on the world. But not for long, for seconds only, a brief collision with the awful present, that terrifying, unnecessary world she now decided to avoid for the rest of her days.

Then she stood, Susan Crumly, rubbing her cheeks once with her knuckles. 'Silly woman. Silly.'

And she began her slow walk back, her head clearer than she could ever remember.

I have said my prayer. I have my absolution. I have decided to confer this freedom on myself.

She had to be getting back to work – a heavenly thought now. In an empty shop window she stopped and looked at her reflection, the face of the new Susan, she remarked to herself, a woman about to embark on the rest of her life, the world would be saddened to learn. I have a jaded look, my skin is pale and my hair – how ragged and dull. And since this last aspect of myself displeases me, I shall do something about it: away with this tired mess. All of it!

SEVEN

The late summer days oozed away. On the radio and in newspapers excitable academics offered serious pronunciations about the disappearing ozone layer that was causing the perpetually recurring unseasonal sunshine. They spoke, too, of the melting ice-caps that would make London a seaside resort by the year 2050. Michael fidgeted in his studio, listening to the radio. He had little work to do and knew he should advertise again to get new commissions, but he had slipped into the throes of a pleasant lassitude, allowing himself to drift a little for the first time in his business life, reinforcing his wish for languor with the repeated affirmation that in less than three years' time he would be forty years old. He read a long book about French salon painting and turned away telephone requests for scarcely profitable small jobs. There was a sense of stolen luxury in this working hiatus, and he enjoyed it, feeling it to be a time of recovering strength, healing. A well-earned break, he told himself, though he intimated nothing to Susan about his inactivity. He set out for the studio each morning at the usual time and returned in the afternoon no earlier than before.

One evening he was even later than usual, having lingered by the radio for an update on the news of a gruesome murder story he had been following for two days. Half-way through an account of the dramatic capture of a gunman in a Birmingham suburb, Michael became suddenly bored with the whole thing and switched off the set to go home. Seconds after leaving his studio he stopped in front of a television and video hire shop, drawn there by a vague noise, a familiar sound that seemed to call him out of the knots of people making their way home from work. He stood at the window and stared at the twenty or so different-sized screens. On each one a man was talking, being interviewed, his face looking to the side at his interrogator. He was a small-eyed handsome creature whom Michael had seen on television many times in his life – once he had presented a popular children's magazine programme. Michael could not remember his name, nor could he hear what he was saying. For some fantastic reason he began to believe the man was talking about Susan. He stepped back on the pavement, the thick rush-hour traffic behind him. How could this be so? What were those words tripping from between that man's meanly parted thin lips? Infidelity? Whore? This last offered with the minute flexion of an eyebrow? Michael stepped up to the window and pressed his fingertips on the smooth glass. The picture changed and credits rolled to signal the end of the programme.

He hurried away, wondering if he should say something to Susan about this, then deciding against it, fearing her ridicule, her attitude towards him sinking even lower than it might already be. He walked quickly, buttoning his jacket against a sudden squall of rain that seemed to fall from a clear blue sky.

Susan was already home. She trilled greetings from the kitchen as he removed his damp jacket in the hall. A vague instinct told him that he should try and avoid her for a while. He grunted his response to her and went upstairs to take a bath.

He lay in the water, motionless, listening to Susan moving busily in the rooms beneath. She shunted a chair, boiled the kettle in the kitchen, rattled knives in a drawer, cursed softly – oh bother. Her husband listened with rapt concentration to each of these sounds, picturing her vividly in his mind, the clothes she was wearing – an Indian block-print skirt and an old black T-shirt – and where she was in either of the two rooms, the rear lounge or the kitchen. The smell of the sprouts and beef she was cooking filtered up the stairs and through the half-open bathroom door, mingling with the steam and the slight perfume from his bath. This was a meal he would not share, since he often lied about having eaten during the afternoon, preferring a late meal which he would make for himself. When she seemed to be shuffling along the hall to the front room, her 'parlour', Michael lifted himself up and leaned over the edge of the bath, his ear inclined towards the talcum-dusty tiled floor, irritated that he could not hear her since she was in the most distant part of the house.

At last, after more than an hour, he got out of the cold water that was beginning to petrify his muscles. For a further fifteen minutes he crouched on the bathroom floor, his face flushed with blood, poised above the peach and white-flecked tiles. She was sitting in the armchair in the rear lounge now, he thought, directly beneath him. She must have eaten, for now he could hear the low tones of Radio 4 and the rustling of a newspaper or magazine. His attention slipped a gear and he wondered about his gunman in the murder story he had been following. He stood, dried what little vapour remained from his cold body, and took his dressing-gown from the bedroom, fastening it loosely as he went downstairs.

Susan smiled. Everything seemed perfectly normal. 'You've been a long time,' she remarked brightly.

'I have, haven't I?' Michael replied with an involuntary little laugh. 'I must have been exceptionally grubby.'

'Did you clean the bath with that new stuff I bought?' asked Susan.

'Yes. I mean, no. I'll do it before I go to bed. I'd forgotten about the new stuff, to be quite honest.' He stood in the centre of the room, a raciness in his head. He wondered if he might be about to faint.

'I'll do it if you like. In fact,' she said, sitting forward, 'I could go up now.'

'No!' Michael said, unintentionally loudly. 'I mean, I can see you're busy. I will do it. Honestly I will.'

'All right. If you insist.'

Michael sat down on the chesterfield, feeling the dizziness converting itself into a headache.

Susan resumed the cleaning of her thimble collection which she had assembled on a low folding table in front of her. Her mouth was tight with renewed concentration. She was wearing her spectacles, which Michael had always felt were for adornment only, and an item of apparel that he had not imagined when he had tried to picture her appearance earlier. He watched her turning knots of tissue inside the thimbles, her brown eyes peeking through the glasses poised on the tip of her narrow nose. She had not bothered with this odd hobby for a long time. She had over three hundred pieces, from holidays abroad, gifts from her parents, friends, some being of the finest porcelain, others of a quite worthless plastic cast. Each had a design of some kind – an intricate coat of arms, fine and minute impressions of dogs, a shepherdess, orchids, tiny maps of Malta, Andalusia, the Cotswolds. When they had first planned their house together, it had been one of Susan's wishes that Michael should make ten narrow shelves to house her collection in the recess beside the chimney breast in the 'parlour'. The effort had cost him days of work on a valuable commission, but he had not revealed this to her.

Watching her now, he felt irritated by her slight,

vigorous activity, feeling that she was deliberately ignoring him, preferring to be absorbed by her tinkling souvenirs. He cleared his throat, opening his mouth without knowing what was going to come out. 'Tell me something,' he said. 'Tell me about human acquisitiveness. What part of you is appeased by "collecting" things? What satisfaction can anyone get from holding say, a thimble, a coin, a book, a picture, a number of these things? What compensation for life's disagreeability can be had from stockpiling "things"? You can never be content, surely. You can't have every thimble in the world.'

He heard his own voice, each of his words, but he could not quite believe what he had said.

Susan picked up another thimble and began rubbing hard, apparently unperturbed by this attack on her simple sense of pleasure. 'I'm not sure what you mean,' she said, after a while. She squinted at a white, metal-topped piece with the letter 'S' copper-plated on its side. 'It's just an instinct, I suppose. It's common in most people. Perhaps it's a microcosmic extension of the capitalism you're rather fond of reminding me I was born to,' she added, her voice heavy with a sarcasm that shocked Michael. 'Have you never collected things?'

'No. I haven't.'

'Not even when you were a child?'

'No, not even then. I don't see the point in it. That's my argument. I want you to tell me what the aim is in hoarding piles of artefacts.'

'I hardly think it's worth discussing. I've explained as much as I know. It's a harmless enough pastime, isn't it?'

Michael said nothing, surprised yet by the floating anger he was experiencing, a disapproval without foundation, an oddly unattached excitement. He looked away from her, knowing that he really wanted to snatch her 'things' from her.

'There,' she exclaimed. 'Finished at last.'

She rubbed her hands and wrapped the thimbles in a large clean cotton square, making a chinking tramp's bundle which she set aside near Michael's bare feet while she folded up the table and slid it behind her chair, not bothering to take it to its usual storage place in the larder. Michael glanced down at the hated parcel on the carpet.

'I think I'll go up now,' Susan said, taking off her glasses, yawning and stretching, Michael watching her every minute movement with unswerving attention.

'Yes. I think I'll come too,' he said.

He bounded from his seat and locked the doors before following his wife up the stairs. He hung around outside the bathroom door while she cleaned her teeth, washed, prepared for bed.

Later, she eased him on to his side, making no comment about his obvious tension, pressing herself against him in the dark room. He sensed her quiet, concentrating hunger, thinking how easily he might succumb to her wish for the close familiar moulding of their bodies. 'I shall have what I want from you,' she whispered in a mockingly officious tone. But he could not respond. He became more tense than ever, annoyed by her touch, certain that he should not give in to her, feeling that to do so might result in some dreadful loss he could not define: some part of his dignity, perhaps, his idea of himself, the individual he thought himself to be.

She squeezed his thigh, then relaxed. 'No?' she asked.

He gave a little snort in reply.

'As you wish,' she said, in her normal voice. 'Actually, I'm rather tired too.' And she turned away from him, her hand trailing along his naked body for one last time. Within minutes her breathing was soft and regular, but Michael did not sleep for a long time.

EIGHT

The new pink and purple carpet was powdered with sawdust. Polythene-wrapped, chromium-framed chairs and planished-metal tables were stacked in bulky piles in one corner of the cellar rooms. Drills mimicked wasps at a windowpane, hammers tapped sporadically, and an electrician on a step-ladder fed grey flex into a hole in the ceiling like a surgeon carefully replacing an artery. Michael stood among the debris, wishing he had not come – it would have waited another day. 'Mr Crumly! Michael! My artist friend. Come over here.' Michael stepped over a cluster of short planks and cast tools towards the half-finished bar where De Lacy was nodding his small bald head in a quickly resumed conversation with a young man in a dark striped suit. He handed a fold of papers to the man who packed them in his briefcase and left.

'Good to see you again,' said De Lacy, suddenly surfacing from some momentary deep thought. 'My discothèque!' He gestured with an expansive sweep of his short arm. 'It is looking very good, yes? Will you come here with your wife when it is finished? For wine, a good meal, a little dancing?'

'Maybe,' said Michael.

De Lacy's smile disappeared in an instant. He embraced Michael lightly, his hands pressed against the younger's upper arms. 'Come. We have to talk business. My time is full of business. Lots of deals to be made. Same with you, yes?'

'Sometimes.'

Michael trailed the little man through pools of warm light made by the spotlights in the ceiling. They passed under a white archway and into a recessed room. 'My carvery,' De Lacy remarked, gravely. 'All good food will be available here,' he added, as if imparting secret information, near-emotional in his aside.

Michael's four paintings were arranged against a long, rough-textured white wall, standing like tombstones, waiting for hanging. They looked small here, alien to Michael's eye. De Lacy scratched his wiry eyebrow with an index finger, his gaze lingering ponderously on the work. 'I'm afraid I have to say that I am not altogether happy, Michael. There are things here that trouble me. This, for instance.' He pointed to the second of the series, a brown landscape with a yellow tractor, small and distant, high on a hillside, leaning at a perilous angle, its cabin doors flung open (each of the four had this kind of theme). 'Maybe it is not precisely what I had in mind. The colours here,' he jabbed his fat thumb at the dark foot of the picture, 'are very dull. Yes? My customers will want something brighter. Too much art here. Too much to think about. People don't want to think when they are enjoying themselves. When they are thinking too much they worry about their responsibilities, about work the next morning, the mortgage, the repairs for their cars. They are not relaxed. They remember too much about who they are. They feel guilty about spending money. Isn't that the case? You are a businessman like myself. You can tell me if this is not so?' He winked at Michael and smiled conspiratorially.

'This is what you asked for,' Michael said, his heart beating apace. 'You gave me the pictures you said you wanted and I have reproduced them quite faithfully, to

47

scale, with the right colours, perhaps even brighter than your pictures. I see I should have brought them with me to remind you of your request.' He looked at the floor, knowing how he loathed confrontation like this, how hopeless he was at putting his own case.

De Lacy stroked his chin with pinched thumb and forefinger. He turned and barked an order to two carpenters behind the new serving hatch, then glared again at Michael's work, shaking his head.

'What did we say? For price?'

'The price is seventeen hundred.'

'I'll give you half.'

'No. The price is . . .'

'Nine hundred. I am not a satisfied man. You must be able to see that. I'm a very unhappy customer.'

'I want,' Michael began, his jaw rigid, his arms quivering, 'the full, contractually agreed price. The cost of these paintings is seventeen hundred pounds.'

'Look at the quality of the paint. When things get rough in here and the drinks start to fly . . .'

'The paint is fine,' Michael said, feeling very unhappy in himself, his stomach growling badly, a small pain lifting from his chest to his head.

'If I do not want them, who will have them?' said De Lacy. 'Eleven-fifty. Generous for poor work. Yes?'

A warm sweat began to tickle in Michael's scalp, breaking on his forehead and temples. He felt dizzy, a radiating heat threatening to engulf him. He wobbled on his feet and felt contractions in his throat. 'I'm sorry,' he said, in a whispering voice he deeply regretted, 'I feel a little unwell.'

De Lacy coughed up a small, unsympathetic laugh. 'Money, my dear friend. The truth of it hurts, yes? Makes you feel sick, though you want it more than anything on earth.' He chuckled. 'Look how thin you are, Crumly. You should come here the night I open. I will give you a big meal, such as you haven't had for a long time, I will bet. You need fattening up, my friend.'

'I have to get outside,' Michael said, gulping the dusty air of the basement.

'Oh, don't go!' De Lacy implored. 'We have so much business to discuss. Actually, for myself, I rather like your work. You do good things. Maybe I will pay you the full seventeen if you do something for the entrance hall?'

Michael turned to go, taken by his malaise.

'When do you come to speak with me again?' bawled the little man when Michael was already at the archway to the room. 'Do I hear from you soon?'

'Yes. Soon,' Michael said, not bothering to look back, knowing De Lacy could not have heard him.

The businessman shook his head, laughed, then dealt sharp instructions to his workers.

Out on the hot street Michael sat down on a low wall, forcing himself to remain upright, pushing his back against the railings behind him. He felt the unseasonal heat rising from the pavement and the deafening traffic seemed to be driving straight into his head. He could taste soap in his mouth.

After a few minutes he stood, shakily, and began walking back in the direction from which he had come. How he rued having made this call. A stern letter might have produced a more effective, certainly a less painful, response from this difficult man. He should go back to his studio, now, immerse himself in new work, revitalize his own commercial affairs, for there was something in De Lacy's attitude that he recognized as being essential to business survival. But he did not.

At a junction in the road, without thinking, he opened the rear door of a taxi and climbed in, not caring to check whether or not the cab was free. He mumbled his home address to the back of the driver's head and, once there, he went to bed, slipping immediately into a fevered sleep, troubled by a dream in which he was being pursued by De Lacy who was wearing a huge white collar and a ridiculous striped tie. Michael ran down a long tunnel, crying out for Susan. He woke several times, pressing his hand on her side of the bed, wishing she were there.

The next day, a Saturday, without telling Susan, he made an appointment to see his doctor.

Hay was a lean, elderly man, with a deeply lined face given to scowling. His smile seemed unnatural, lips almost non-existent, dentures creamy and straight. Michael shuffled in the chair. He had felt very uneasy in the waiting-room amidst juvenile, autumnal coughs and the old with their elaborate descriptions of their truly profound ailments. The reason he had selected for his visit – his poor digestion – seemed to have disappeared. Feeling foolish, suddenly possessing a vague wisdom and insight, he realized, as he often did on the number of times that he had visited there, that his presence in this gloss-green painted room was simply the result of a compulsion, a need to 'see someone'. His stomach pains now seemed no more than a wilful contrivance, a phantom suffering.

'So,' said the doctor, eyeing the note-filled card that constituted Michael's medical history. 'You are here again, Michael.'

'My stomach, this time. I believe I may have consulted you about it before. Last year?'

Hay let the card fall to the desk top. He looked up at Michael. 'May,' he said. 'This year. Five months ago.'

'Really? I hadn't realized. You must be sick of seeing me,' Michael ventured with a small laugh.

Five months ago, he now recalled, Susan had gone away for three days to a company exhibition in Bristol. His visit here then had also been made without her knowledge. He had not wanted her to go to Bristol, harbouring many secret misgivings about who she was going with, where she would be staying. He had loudly challenged the value of the exhibition. But out of respect for their 'freedom' policy he had intimated none of his true fears. Now he wondered, briefly, about the connection between his small dread of her going away and his appearance here then, which he had, until now, forgotten completely.

'Then,' the doctor said, looking down at his notes, 'you described a "burning pain" in, I have recorded here, the diaphragm region of your abdomen. Your words. Now you tell me you have a "griping" pain in the pit of your stomach. I don't wish to seem pedantic, but the precise words a patient uses are often crucial to a doctor's diagnosis. Do you have this new pain now?'

'Not as this particular moment. But it was very bad this morning. My wife would be able to testify to that.'

Hay smiled, the lines multiplying in his unappealing face. 'You are not on trial, Michael, I have no need for independent witnesses to testify to the veracity of your claim.' The two smiled in unison. 'What does concern me,' he continued, 'is that when someone comes to see me, especially a younger man like yourself, a rare visitor as a rule, it is because they are troubled by something. It is not necessarily the ailment itself, rather it might be the consequences of the illness or perhaps its causes; especially, I believe, the way it interferes with the sufferer's life and his equable state of mind. Do you understand me?'

'I'm not sure . . .'

'Is there,' Hay ventured, leathery flesh gathering in rolls above his raised eyebrows, 'possibly some other reason why you might have come to see me?'

Michael shrank in his chair, looking at the space between his feet, feeling the weight of his identity, his own presence, crushing him down. He could not answer. And then he realized that this same man, just seven weeks before, had dealt with Susan's pregnancy – 'Briefly. Sensibly,' she had said. Suddenly his mind was shot through with absurd images of this old racka-bones attending to his prone, naked wife. What might have gone on between these two? Nothing. Of course, nothing.

'No. No other reason. My stomach is bad, that's all. If there was anything else, I would tell you.'

'Are you sure?'

'Must I invent another motive to satisfy you?'

'Certainly not. Forgive me. I have to explore every avenue, I'm sure you understand.'

Michael said nothing, sensing a rare victory for his part in this exchange.

The doctor became very still for a few moments, looking down thoughtfully into the small space between him and his patient. Still hoping, Michael thought, that I will break.

'Very well then . . .' said Hay, and he prescribed an antacid that he said was new on the market and which he had been reassured had shown remarkable results in clinical trials. Michael was to return in a fortnight if his stomach had not improved.

Michael passed back through the busy waiting-room, self-consciously clutching the prescription sheet, the ill-gotten prize of which he now felt inexplicably ashamed. He stepped out into the street where a sharp breeze lifted the thing from his fingers. He chased it along the pavement, tears welling that he could not understand.

NINE

Susan walked slowly away from the low entrance to Peterborough station, her travel bag scraping against her knees, and climbed into a taxi standing at the head of a long row of waiting vehicles. She spoke the address brightly to the driver, masking the usual slight depression which always affected her spirit when she visited her parents. The concept of 'home', of duty, unwanted obligations, disturbed her. She felt selfish, realizing that she might prefer to have none of these ties. And yet there was another preoccupation, beneath the surface of her waking life, that the child she had been resided in her yet, somehow drew her back to the remembered comfort of this place, away from Michael and the house they shared, away from her job, away from the adult – that other being who frightened her sometimes – that she had become simply, it seemed, by virtue of the passing of time.

The car wheeled into the slow traffic, taking her beneath the witnessing frown of the cathedral, through mazes of roadworks, over the Nene, and past one of the two factories her father owned. She looked impassively at the murrey-coloured, corrugated source of, and monument to, her father's wealth. The linear features of each of the six joined-together buildings were picked out in canary yellow and each of these outsize shoe-boxes was big enough to house a church. For this place she felt no sense of pride, no gratitude;

she could not preen herself on her father's obvious success. Rather, she would often think about the people her father employed, the small lives she secretly envied, those easily defined, limited existences, innocuous, easily given to joy, she imagined, people unconcerned with ambition, the illusion of 'fulfilment' that had been drummed into her consciousness and that of the other girls at her public school. But when she had grown up, Susan only feigned ambition, selecting a mundane job, working hard at it, wanting little else, believing she had no talent for success, embarrassed by the prospect of one day – a time yet decades away, she deeply hoped – inheriting her parents' wealth. When that day came, she had envisaged taking one tour of her premises, perhaps patronizing the workers by having lunch in the canteen, before turning the whole company over to the family solicitor to get the highest price he could. Her father must surely be expecting this, though she dreaded the day when they might engage in formal discussions about the dissection of his empire after his death. In her own fashion, she believed she had created something like the factory workers' lives, a satellite existence, without true anxieties, a small life, happy, really. And so much of this had been thanks to Michael, dull Michael, worrying, taciturn, dear Michael.

The car took her up the small steep drive to the grey-beige growling Victorian lump that had encased so much of her lonely childhood.

Her mother, Eileen Thorpe, was draped across the arms of a deep chair in the big, airy lounge, a tray at her side, sport on the television. 'I do like that Peter whatsisname. He's quite yummy,' she said by way of greeting, her eyes not swerving from the screen, her mouth full of cake. She wrung her sticky fingers on a cloth from the tray.

Susan tossed her bag beside the sofa, kicked off her

shoes and flopped down on the soft, brown velvet cushions.

'Who?' she asked.

'This chap. No, not him. The one with the moustache. The presenter or the link man or whatever they call them.' Susan's mother watched a great deal of television, yet always made a point of not being able to remember the names of the people she saw. She took another bun from the plate on the tray. 'These pastries are villainous. Like all good things, I suppose they clog the platelets or something. Want one?'

'Not for me. Thank you,' Susan replied, stirring herself to pour coffee from the blue-flowered pot at her mother's side, taking her already used cup, knowing there would be no objection to this small act of indolence.

'So, how was your journey?' Eileen asked, routinely, forcedly. 'It seems ages since we last saw you. Tony said that just the other evening before he zoomed off to some whizz-bang deal he was putting together in Notts.'

'I suppose I've been quite busy. Work and all that,' said Susan, noting to herself how successfully she could evade thoughts about her recent 'difficulty'. No more guilt? So soon? 'I'm sorry.'

'Silly. Don't apologize,' said Eileen, turning towards her with one of her random, pointed stares. 'Live your life, my dear. Live it to the full. Why should you worry about boring old insects like Tony and me? We should hate you to worry about us.'

Susan watched her devour another cake then light a Rothmans, her pliant long fingers flapping smoke from around her face. In the fine light of brief sunshine, Susan noted how her mother's hair had always remained the most stubborn pale gold. Her nails were bitten short and she always wore make-up, expertly and subtly applied, even now, when it was clear she

55

had probably been nowhere that morning and was unlikely to be budging from the house all day. Her skin was dry, though; taut and shiny on her high cheek-bones, though the colour was natural and good. Many in the Midlands middle-classes, the professional and managerial sets, envied Eileen her elegance, the devil-can-go-hang-himself attitude she seemed, overtly, to bring to every aspect of her self-indulgent life.

And yet, thought Susan, who among those taffeta-gowned, silk-shirted bodies that fawned over her at cocktail parties, that celebrated her uninhibited black humour and mild heresy, who among them would ever have believed that, ten years ago, her mother had driven herself to the East Anglia coast and thrown herself to the sea? Only Susan knew the tale, certainly true, of that cold, secret day, and of the three strong waves – just my luck, a bloody miracle, her mother had said – that came in succession to throw her back on to the rocks. She yet carried a scar where the jagged stone had torn her hip. Cursing the fates that conspired against her, she had picked herself up and driven back home, dripping wet, had dried herself, changed her clothes, shrugged off the only fundamental gesture she had made in her life, and succumbed, tight-lipped, to a desperate influenza that would not lift for a month. Now she watched satellite television, the world around her, the shapeless, passing years, never once offering any serious rumination about life.

'You eat too much rubbish,' Susan said. 'You'll get heart disease.'

'Don't be bourgeois, there's a dear. I get enough of that at Tony's vile company receptions. True, I might go purple for ten minutes and depart this life, but, so what? It might be better on the other side. It must be good – no one's ever come back to tell us what it's like,' said Eileen, with a wry smile, eyelids hooded. 'What do you think?'

'I don't know what to think. I'm like you really, I prefer not to think about it at all.'

'Bravo! Quite right! Danish pastry?'

'No, thank you.'

Susan closed her eyes and slipped, unwillingly, into the seductive trance that she always experienced when she came back home. She tried to avoid it, to deny the cloying child who came back to life in her, teasing and enticing her from her belief that, at thirty-two, to adhere still to one's parents was immature. Soon, though, she knew she would go and look in her old room, perhaps even ring Michael, if the feeling became too strong, to say she would be staying the night. She was sliding, sliding . . . The luxury of being cared for again! The hiving away of all personal responsibilities . . . She opened her eyes and looked at her mother: another girl, fifty-three years old, mischievous, idling in the fruits of her husband's success as she had since she was seventeen.

'Where is Daddy?'

'Out. Somewhere.' Eileen squinted at her fingers, admiring a hangnail before she bit it away. 'I think he has a new lover.'

'Has he?' asked Susan, alerted by the remark. 'Anyone we might know?'

'I believe', her mother began with an adolescent giggle, 'she is a lady mineralogist.' She rubbed her hands. 'God knows where he finds them these days. What his boardroom cronies must think of it all I do not know.'

'Doesn't it ever get to you?'

Her mother screwed herself round in the chair to face the television again. She flicked through the channels with the remote control. 'Doesn't what ever get to me?'

'His infidelity. His adultery. Call it what you like.'

'Adultery is a very heavy, loaded word, dear daughter. Tony and I decided a long time ago that we ought not to have married. For us, I think, wedlock is little more than a moral system, well, immoral in our case. Nowadays, with both of us knocking on a bit, it's just a matter of being sensible, really. It is terribly convenient for us both to remain married. He provides the money, amply and without question, and I keep his barn of a house and tag along with him to dinners, conferences, what-have-you, generally keeping myself decorous, acerbically humoured, indifferent to it all, even the sniggers of his friends-in-the-know.' She lit another cigarette. 'If something hurts me, I think it's that – the assumptions of those overgrown golfing schoolboys who don't understand our relationship. When they've lived long enough . . .' Her voice trailed away. She looked to the french windows where rain had begun spattering heavily, beating the glass like many drumming fingers. 'How is Michael?' she asked. 'Is he still slim, quiet, desirable? I always fancied him, you know,' she teased.

'He's been in an odd sort of mood lately. More withdrawn than ever. I can't seem to please him.'

'Well, why bother?' Eileen rapped, quickly adding, perhaps regretting the suddenness of her rejoinder, 'He'll come round. They always do. They must have their little phases to go through. Is he working too hard?'

'I don't think so. The other day, when he could be bothered to speak to me, he said that things were quiet at the moment. Estate agents use printed cardboard signs now . . .'

'God, they're such philistines.'

'The competition is stiff all round, he reckons. New firms, keen, bold, ambitious, and Michael's such a slowcoach.'

'Tony would give him a job, if he wanted one. He's remarked on it before. And it would pay well, I'd see to that.'

'Michael would hate working for someone else again. I wouldn't want him to. It might change him into something I didn't want him to be.'

'How wise you are. I can quite understand what you mean.'

Susan yawned and stretched, succumbing, willingly now, to the comfort and ease afforded by the big familiar house and her mother's laconic, reassuring presence. 'I feel rather sleepy. Would you be offended if I took a little nap?'

'Susan dear, this is your home. Do as you please. Anyway, snooker's on in a minute and I would prefer that my concentration was not disturbed.'

In the silent, elysian atmosphere of her room, the daughter of the house climbed beneath a cherry-patterned duvet and closed her eyes again. But she did not sleep for long, a few minutes, if at all. She stared at the powder-pink walls through half-open eyes, and a high lilac scraped drily at the window, its whip-thin branches losing the last of its foliage, dried curled leaves suspended by threads, turning in the breeze like spinning pupae. Susan's infant self would not truly come to life.

In this room she had first made love to Michael. There had been others – an intense and boring youth from her college who had harangued her father for his wealth and who had left Susan feeling, briefly, invaded and abused. Then there had been Derek Rodney who owned an eighteenth of his father's Midlands brewery, who had fumbled with her clothing like a fourteen-year-old, sucking at her skin with cold, heavy lips, and who was now an MP indifferently holding a minute majority in a northern town which he would surely be happy to lose in the next general election. But Michael had been so different. Brooding, nervous Michael Crumly, his white skin moist and cool to her touch – for him she could make her heart capacious. How she had devoured him! Heavens above! 'He's a wiry thing,' her mother had said when she first saw him. 'Receding too. Already . . .'

Scrambling in the high vault of her memory, Susan recalled the first time she had seen him, that slight, urgent presence, carefully manipulating the elaborate company motifs he had made for her employer's trade exhibition. She had hardly noticed him for an hour, busy as she was setting out forms and pamphlets for the salesmen, unwrapping her typewriter, glancing up at him with detached interest. She sensed, even then, a coolness about him, a steady judgement of people and situations. He seemed to come from another world – he was scarcely a 'type', someone you could pigeonhole. 'Looks serious, doesn't he?' remarked her friend, Glenda Telford. 'Quite your sort, Sue, I would think.'

'Really?'

'Want a meeting?' her friend had asked with fire in her round eyes.

'No! Please. I mean, he may be married. Glenda . . .'

But her colleague was already tapping the thin young man on his shoulder, laughing, making him blush to his open shirt collar. She's taking him for herself, Susan thought. And she can have him if she's in such need. In fact Michael, politely, in embarrassment, declined to speak to Susan, painstakingly ignoring her as he wriggled on his step-ladders, screwing his signs on to the cubical wall. A long time ago, Susan felt.

Four weeks later she had seen him for the second time. He was red-faced, not with embarrassment or exertion, but with a bile in his blood that would not move. He had stormed into the company's offices, demanding to know, in a low and insistent voice, why his account had not been settled in full. The office manager, unused to clients appearing in person, shuffled to Susan's desk with the angry man. He asked her to find the Crumly account. 'Crumly, Crumly,' she repeated, thumbing through the sheaves of paper at her side, smiling involuntarily. Crumly – such a homely, modest name. All she knew of Yorkshire, its limestone speckled moors and dales, its withering dark industrial towns, its stoical self-effacing people with their gravy-laden accent, could be summed up in 'Crumly'. She adored it, instantly. It filled her with hunger, drew her the way pictures in a book or brochure give the mind a yearning for travel, for ownership of a new life, new peoples. 'Crumly': it made her want to laugh out loud. 'It's not here. I shall have to check upstairs. It must already have gone to accounts for payment. If you could wait here a moment, Mr Crumly.'

'I'd like to come with you,' he said, further revealing the slight obsession that was inspiring him.

'If you wish.'

The anxious man, nervous as a sparrow in the hand, trailed her to the upstairs accounts window.

'C-R-U-M-L-Y.' The girl disappeared into the back rooms of the office, Michael watching her go, his eyes yet taken by the space she had occupied behind the window. Moments passed. Susan smiled at him, a smile he returned, an automatic, sheepish response caused partly by his deep unease with this place, with his reason for being here.

'Tell me what you sell here,' he asked suddenly. 'I've never really understood.'

'Oh, financial advice, insurance, equities, investment schemes, you name it.'

'Non-things,' he said with a quivering laugh.

'Yes. Abstractions,' Susan agreed. 'Sometimes I wish we sold brushes or house bricks. It would have more meaning to people like me.'

The girl returned. 'I have the cheque here. It will be posted to you this afternoon. First class.'

'I'd like to take it now, please. The date for payment

was the second, not the fifth,' he said breathlessly, yet with certainty in his voice.

'I'm not sure if I can do that. I'll need identification. '

'I will vouch for him,' Susan said.

She stood and watched him leaving, pausing at the top of the stairs, his anxiety visibly appeased now. And she knew without a shadow of a doubt, having no right to such a powerful knowledge, that he would turn and ask her to go out one evening. What a quiet small eternity that was. Such an effort it must have taken for this fearful, hardy soul, sweat prickling on his pale receding forehead, eyes drawn back into his skull, to make that small request. 'Of course, any time you like,' Susan had replied briskly, in imitation of her friend Glenda who would not have paused so long.

Fourteen weeks later, in this house, alone in this room, on the morning of her wedding, Susan had felt a supremacy over her destiny for the first time in her life, knowing she was applying an ultimate design to her existence in this world. It was a sensible transaction, she thought, in her most sober moments. In time it might prove to be no more than that. But they had both quickly realized that they might make each other content, rapidly laying down plans for creating a safe place, a haven from the world they agreed threatened them both, though in different ways. And yet how often had she worried that she might merely be trying to compete with her parents' fractured relationship, to make a success of something they could not?

At the wedding Michael had seemed just the same as always, gloomy and defenceless, his brown suit hanging from his taut skeleton, wrists dangling from awry shirt cuffs. Still, he had an almost feline grace, a subtlety and grim sense of precision that Susan had discovered in him, an abiding power that he might have converted into achievement had he been ambitious, which she was relieved he showed no signs of becoming. Susan knew he could never easily escape his vulnerability, the self-possession she had seen and adored immediately.

In the registry office with its long walnut table laid out like an altar with yellow plastic chrysanthemums at either end, she had wanted to laugh out loud, enraptured by the simplicity, the sheer indisputability of the act. On the steps outside he smiled for photographs, clinging to her, trailing his older brother Ben, the token best man. That night, while he slumbered heavily, she could not sleep for the sheer exhilaration of it all, her sense of responsibility towards someone else, the first in her life. And in the months that followed she applied her physical love by system, besotted by different parts of this creature she owned, the hips she could squeeze, the hollows in his shoulders, his long wriggly toes with their tiny nails, the cavity beneath the soft stomach where she would stray her fingers and he might shrink away – what reticence! such shyness! – and the limbs in the tumbled sheets which she would stroke while he slept . . . Her dutifulness had never deserted her, she decided, not even during these last few months when they had been so cool and distant with each other. This she thought as the telephone rang in some distant corner of her parents' house, this home of the many small ghosts of her life 'before Michael'.

Her mother called from the foot of the stairs, her voice resonant of an ancient past. 'Susan? Sue? It's for you. Your delectable husband.'

Susan sat upright and threw back the duvet, feeling a small sudden vexation that Michael should ring her here, disturb her from her enriching reveries. She skipped down the stairs in her stockinged feet, the dutiful daughter running at her mother's bidding. The receiver lay prone on a marble-topped table in the hall. 'Michael?'

'Thank God. You're all right then?'

'Of course I'm all right. Why shouldn't I be?'

'There's been a rail accident. An Edinburgh train. I thought it might be yours. Oh dear God, you're safe.'

Susan frowned. 'What accident? I haven't heard of any accident.'

'This morning. I heard it on the radio. A newsflash.' The tone of his voice became plain, insistent. 'I heard it, Susan.'

'Well, I'm OK. So you needn't worry.'

'But that's just it. I have been worrying,' said her husband, his voice rising again. 'You can't imagine how worried I've been. You didn't tell me when you would be back. Are you staying overnight?'

'I haven't decided yet. I was thinking about it.'

'No!' he cried. Then seeming to control himself: 'Please don't stay. Come home. I've been out of my mind thinking about you. There's a train at 6.18 from your end. You could have tea with Tony and Eileen, then catch that.'

Susan bit her lip, frankly irritated by Michael's gravity and sense of urgency, those distractions she could sense at the other end of the line, a hundred miles away. And he had checked on the times of the trains. Usually, before, he would have been quite keen that she went away for the occasional weekend – he used to love his own company so much. Why could she not believe a word about this 'accident'? She thought herself despicable for not trusting him, for thinking he might be making all this up. In an instant she reflected on all she felt she might owe him, on the quiet torment he must have endured over the last few months, on the anguish to which he could not give voice, such was his way. The mistake she had made, that idiotic mistake with those damned pills.

'Susan?'

'I'll be home this evening,' she said, adding impassively: 'Don't take on so.'

She heard the small sigh. His relief was almost tangible. 'I'll be waiting.'

Susan insisted that he said goodbye, then replaced the receiver, pressing it hard into its cradle.

In the lounge her mother was watching downhill skiing, chocolates an arm's length away. Susan felt an inexplicable envy for her mother's hedonistic, loveless existence, a new insight into the fact that her parents, for all their mutual duplicity, still seemed to know where they stood with each other, in an unlikely way. 'Problems?' asked Eileen.

'Michael's a little unwell,' she lied, not knowing why.

'Oh, the poor sweet. You must go to him and comfort him. He needs you. He needs mothering . . .'

'I'm not his mother,' Susan snapped.

'Sorry. I didn't mean . . .'

'Never mind.'

Susan began looking about for her things.

'Mother?' she asked. 'Have you been watching the news?'

'Why, yes. There's been the most awful train crash. Dozens perished, they believe.'

Susan closed her eyes, her whole being flooding with relief. How she would make amends with Michael. She might even confess her wicked failure to believe him. She would leave immediately. 'Where?'

'Somewhere. Let me think. Was it the South of France? Yes, that was it. Marseilles. Wonderful cuisine. You should go there. You'd love it.'

Susan dropped heavily on to the sofa.

'Would I?'

TEN

Michael Crumly dreamed of a field of coarse wheat grown chest-high under a cruelly hot sun. Down the path that divided the land came his wife Susan and her father. Her arm looped around her father's, Susan appeared to be floating in her long, full-skirted purple dress. The father was making great play of attempting to shield his daughter from the heat with a small parasol. Michael ran to meet them, stumbling, picking himself up, never seeming able to shorten the distance that separated him from them. Susan's father leaned down and kissed her cheek lightly. Michael called to them but his voice would not carry on the still air. Susan's father scooped her up in his arms, held her high, watched her turn into a grey bird and fly away. Then he ran into the wheat and was swallowed by it. Michael called again, still believing in their secret presence. He wanted to know why they would not speak with him.

Then he dreamed of a long wooded glade bordered by pillars of silver birch whose branches met to form a green canopy that refined the light cast on the poppy-strewn earth. Two figures ran in and out of the trees. They wore sweeping capes, one red, one yellow, with caps of the same colour that covered their faces. Michael sought them down the flowery avenue, finding one, a woman, her hat tipped over her eyes. He lunged for her – *Now I have you!* – but was left with only the yellow coat and the hat that floated to the ground. The wind carried faint laughter to the treetops.

In his own house Michael saw Susan playing a game in which she lifted her head clean from her shoulders, then replaced it, over and over again. Michael was horrified, but could only laugh.

Then he was transported again, this time seeing legions of ragged infants. His own well-being was repulsive to him, a cause of mortal shame. They were marching along a wet muddy road, refugees from some unknown war. Michael walked with them. They insisted that he drank water with them, their voices vague and pleading. But he could not accept. Then they crowded around him, smothering him, beating him about his head and body with their soft wet claws. He lashed out and saw dark blood, only that.

Now he was sitting quietly in a white room with a high window through which he could see nothing but a fraction of twilight sky. He could hear odd noises of a world at work outside, of machines, of low, mumbled conversations. A uniformed woman came to the room and asked him: 'Does nothing make you happy? You're not the only one, you know.' She left. A man came, then, and asked him serious questions about Susan. Michael wanted to oblige, to give him the facts he knew were in his mind, to get them out of his head. But when he tried to unload his information, his ideas, the confession became lost in an invisible labyrinth between him and his visitor, blocked by impenetrable dead ends, wedged tight in unnegotiable turns. The words that did come out of his mouth were maunder, bore no relation to the great, undefined truths he was harbouring. 'I want to tell you,' he said, 'about the tree that blossoms in winter on whose branches and petals the snow will not rest.' Then he laughed for a long time. The man took offence and left.

Michael had a sensation of waiting then, a waiting

that was an activity in itself, an attendance on nothing he could think of. His dreaming eye splintered from his body, looked down at the corporal Michael who lay in his bed, twitching at odd, earthbound noises. This spirit saw Susan in the bed beside Michael. It wanted to wake them both, to get them to explain themselves. Then it drifted high to a world of space and light, leaving the old Michael absorbed by the darkness below . . .

He woke to hear an early morning thunderstorm rumbling over London like distant shellfire. The rain was falling thick and heavy on the roof of the house, whipping the window like cast gravel, the wind groaning like a loveless old whore. The young professionals and market traders alike ran from their houses, thudding along the pavement to cars, buses, trains. Susan pressed herself against her husband, tracing lines on his arm and thighs with cold fingertips. With a minute movement of his arm Michael signalled his tension, and Susan turned away to face the window. It was still early. She did not go back to sleep. Neither of them did. Nor did they seem to wish to acknowledge their proximity to each other, each possessed now by their individual, lonely selves.

A strange sensation was beginning to burgeon within Michael, threatening to overpower him, taking over his thoughts. He could not describe it to himself, nor did he feel he could suppress it, which worried him. He stared at the dirty light growing on the ceiling, not believing that this odd consciousness newly alive in him had anything to do with his wife, could possibly be connected with her in any way. In a sense, he felt quite happy, light in his whole being, almost euphoric. 'Nothing else matters now,' was an apparently meaningless phrase spinning around in his head. Unable to suppress a smile, he turned his face to the door, feeling a giggling fit which he was able to stifle. Whatever this invading phenomenon was, there seemed one rule which he must obey, a crucially important stricture: Susan must know nothing. Then he lay on his back again. This is silly, he thought.

His wife gave a little moan of weariness and rose from her side of the bed. Michael, hands clasped on his bare smooth chest, watched her dressing. Things are different for women, he thought. They are flexible and autonomous, less prudish than men who find childish ways of distracting themselves from making any true contribution to life with useless work, money, property, changing watery morals, fetishistic sports. Those things, Michael arrogantly believed, are for other men, not me. Those 'others' do not have to be modern to survive, they preserve themselves with their simple avoidance of responsibility. Men can always hide behind a woman's strength, draw their resilience from her, that is why they marry – to seek a new mother, to shelter behind this shield of womanly power, the power a woman like Susan possesses. Michael's mind suddenly teemed with thoughts such as these.

He watched his wife in those awesomely revealing moments, drawn as never before, irresistibly enchanted by the fine curve of her lightly tanned back, the little fatty folds above her hips, her soft knees, her breasts, and the steady poise of her brown animal's eyes which he saw in the dressing-table mirror. He followed each movement as she stooped to pick underwear from the drawer, as she buttoned up her white blouse, as she tugged the zip in the side of her navy skirt and smoothed it into its tight, perfect fit. Such coolness and certainty. Such precision and quiet, practised economy. He became, in those few fateful minutes, suddenly and intensely jealous – not of his wife as an individual, the Susan he knew, his friend Susan, nor of his refined and unspoken sense of being *owned* by her, nor of his own troublesome feeling of *possessing* her (which had been there, dimly residing in his mind since they had first married) – it was none of these obvious things. In those three or four profound minutes, Michael's primary, conflagrating desire, was for Susan's sex, her womanhood. He actually wanted to *be* Susan, to become her, somehow.

She carefully avoided his stare and passed through to the bathroom, then down the stairs.

Michael felt a sudden, chilling fear, the primitive dread of a child whose mother has left the room, the inconsolable dismay of this infant who cannot comprehend that she has not disappeared forever. Not to have his wife with him at that moment became devastatingly unthinkable to Michael. The wind rushed at the roof of the house, shook the window in its frame, then subsided as the last of the rain and the thunder drifted away over the city. Birds pattered and twittered in the gutter. Compelled by his sense of unbearable vulnerability, the grasping fear of being without Susan that he could no more explain than he could fly, Michael jumped naked from the bed and rushed after her.

He found her in the kitchen, efficiently manipulating the controls on the electric cooker. The sight of her filled him with an untrammelled relief. He stood behind her and put his hand in her soft hair, pulling tenderly, fondly stroking the outline of her head. She shrugged with pleasure. 'Don't. Please.' Suddenly, ostensibly disturbed by the intimacy of his small action, he withdrew his hand as quickly as if he had been reaching for a flame.

'I'd prefer it if you didn't go to work today. I'll ring them for you. What's the name of the personnel man? I can tell him you're not well. It won't matter to them.'

What was he saying? Where did this idea come from? He could hear his own calm voice, the certainty of his suggestion, but he could not understand himself.

Susan lifted a saucepan of lapping, hissing milk from

the cooker, holding the hot enamel handle with a tea-towel wrapped around her palm. 'You do look silly,' she said, turning and smiling – such ready smiles she had – as she poured the milk on a sparing quantity of cereal in a dish. 'Why don't you get dressed? You look a little out of place, naked, in the kitchen. I'll open the curtains, then you'll know,' she said, her words tainted with a hint of the old sexual collaboration of their early days together.

'I don't think you understand,' came the mysterious voice from somewhere inside him. 'You're not listening to me.'

Susan put down the towel and turned to face him, embracing him, holding him against her. He winced at the feel of her rough skirt against his nakedness, her blouse against his chest, her hands cupped on his shoulders. 'This evening, if you like,' she purred, 'I could fix a big supper, the way we used to like them. Italian, Chinese. Or French. And we could have wine too. Lots of that. What do you think?'

Michael could see her broad, full-toothed smile, pretty, and yet devilish, inches from his face, the eyes narrowing beneath the crow's-wing brows. He dashed her away from him. 'Don't touch me! Please. I . . . I can't stand it. I don't know what it is. I just don't want you to touch me. All I want is for you to listen to me,' he said, clasping his hands tight in a gesture of frustration. 'I just want you to stay here today. With me. Don't ask why. I don't know why. I simply want you to do as I ask.'

Susan stood her ground one pace away, her face snarled in disbelief. She snatched up her steaming dish and went through to the lounge, seating herself on the chesterfield with one leg tucked beneath her, snatching her food to her mouth with the spoon. The image of the man on the screens in the television shop – forgotten since the day he had first seen it – resurfaced clearly in Michael's mind. I should ask her now about this, he thought. She should tell me. I have a right to know. I am her husband!

He trailed her from the kitchen, drawn again by the centre of his own being which he felt Susan possessed that morning. He hovered over her, then sat down on the armchair, watching her eat. She shook her head, her mouth full of food she no longer wanted. 'You should go back to bed,' she offered, sourly. 'You're just not yourself. You don't make sense these days.'

He laughed. 'I'm all right! I love you, that's all. I just want to talk to you, to be with you, to know what you think of me. Is there anything wrong with that?'

'I don't understand you. Either you can't bring yourself to say a word to me or you want to argue for hours. You pick holes in everything I do. I know things haven't been too good between us lately, but you just won't spit it out. You seem to be foisting all your insecurities . . .'

'My insecurities?'

'Yes, Michael, your insecurities. You put them all over on to me. Sometimes it's as if you want me to confess something, to affirm some wild presumption you seem to have made about me. I wish I knew what it was. I would admit it straight away if I thought it might get you thinking normally again. I don't know what's got into you, Michael,' she said, taking the dish back to the kitchen. She returned through the lounge on her way to the hall. 'I wish you'd pull yourself together. Find a therapist or something.'

What power she had, this being he might want to be, this fragile soul who could crush him so effectively with her remarks. Confused again, frankly affronted by her words, Michael ran back up the stairs, brushing past her as she pulled on her coat. The many thoughts in his mind raced, multiplied, pouring from that hidden obfuscation. Her voice echoed in him yet, and he hated it and wished that he could wrench it from his mind. Now he felt dully subservient to the waywardness that held him. He sat down on the corner of the bed, vainly trying to make sense of what was happening to him. He heard the front door slam and his heart shrank. He stalked the bedroom for his clothes and dressed as quickly as he could, dancing into his trousers, cursing shirt buttons, pushing his bare feet into his shoes. He bounded down the stairs and into the street.

She was not there. He sensed her absence from the poky little road as a grievous loss. He ran on to the end of the street and up into the dog-leg avenue where grey-suited men with raincoats over their arms chattered and strolled to work. A car reversed from a drive. Then another. A stray dog, out for the night, pattered briskly along the pavement, its dry tongue lolling. Without any apparent reason or distraction it careered into the road, its vacant animal mind oblivious of the danger. It ran whimpering, unharmed, from the wheels of a screeching van, to disappear down a garden path.

Michael ran on, weaving along the grass verges until he came to the junction at the end of the avenue. The station was opposite. In his rational mind he knew that Susan would already have boarded the tube to town. Breathless, his throat sore and a taste of iron in his mouth, he glared wild-eyed at the tube station portico, knowing something, now, of his folly, miserable at the hands of his overwhelming urges. He ran his fingers through the rat-tails that passed for his hair and wiped the sweat from his unshaven face – another vagrant facing another day. Then he made the almost insuperable effort of turning back to return to the house.

ELEVEN

A paper world.

Female fingers pecked, and paused, hovering above plastic keyboards. Susan crouched over her own machine, sensing the familiar dull pain of fatigue along the length of her spine, performed the same service for Jupiter Services (UK) plc, looking gloomily at the heap of estimates, invoices, referrals, agreements – the paper currency of her working life – to her left. No end to the things. Never a moment when they were gone and she might say, 'There. Finished.' The clock on the wall, ever four minutes slow, which brought attentive beings here four minutes early and detained them four minutes too long at the end of the day, obstinately refused to sharpen its pace, the red second hand sweeping the white face with ungrudging precision. Fiercesome time. Time to be filled staining pieces of paper plucked from a system of imponderable complexity. Time given from one's life for money received at the end of the month – Thank you, sirs. Much obliged.

Susan arched her back and rubbed her ankles together, stretching her legs under the desk. From behind her came an impish known voice: 'I fear you are committing an unforgivable sin, my dear.'

She turned to face her old friend.

'What sin?'

'Daydreaming, love. Thinking of the universe, or man's cruelty to man, or to you. Whatever. You'll go stir crazy. Just grit your teeth and think of the salary, no matter how meagre it is. It's the only way to stay sane – thinking of material profit. Something on your mind?'

Glenda was quite a stranger in this office, these days. A few months ago she had been whisked Upstairs. To Marketing Strategy, no less, my dear.

'No. I don't think so,' Susan said, weakly, wondering if Glenda could possibly have known about her 'illness'. Dr Hay had written 'post-viral fatigue' on her sick note, inventing a nasty bout of gastro-enteritis which might have brought on this cleverly imagined ailment. How fortunate she had been to have been 'cared for' by such a worldly-wise man. Might a female GP, perhaps with non-medical-curriculum convictions, have been so accommodating? There was a young woman in the same practice. Susan had seen her. She wore a thick coral jumper and espadrilles and from her Susan had often imagined a raised eyebrow, a breathless smile, and the comment offered with criminal naïvety: 'The truth, Mrs Crumly. We must tell your employers the truth. It's nothing to be ashamed of. We must let it be known that women have the right to choose. It is my duty to record "termination of pregnancy", don't you, as a woman, agree?' She would cry a lot, that one, Susan believed. Dr Hay should send her packing, tell her to get some street-sense.

'Tell me Glenda, how is life among the privileged, in the ethereal echelons, the Great Upstairs?'

Her friend settled half a long leg on the side of Susan's desk, leaning towards her with her famous look of pending revelation. She held her tousled fair hair back from her rouged cheeks, thick-beaded purple necklace swaying above her ivory jumper. 'Oh, he is wonderful! Are there any rumours?'

'Who's wonderful? Ted?'

'That lump?'

'He's your husband.'

'No, no, no. We divorced. Where have you been lately?'

'I didn't know that. Divorced when?'

'Well, all right, it's not quite settled yet. Not officially anyway. We still have to dot a few "i"s, cross a few swords, or whatever. You know how it is.' She grinned triumphantly, challenging Susan to accuse her of deceit. Then she offered a defiant glare to the office supervisor, Parkes, who was watching from behind his window at the end of the office. She glistened with mischief. 'His name is Martin.'

'Martin?'

'Sssh! Can't say too much. He's part of the firm.'

'Which part?'

'Provincial.'

'Bristol? Glasgow? Derby?' Susan asked, enjoying the tease and the diversion from her monotonous work. 'I must have heard of him. Do tell.'

'I can't, dear. Simply can *not*. Sworn to secrecy and all that.'

'He must be married then. And others must know. Two minutes ago you were asking me if there were any "noises off".'

'Another indiscretion. A failing of mine. I'm known for it, I fear. Ted always said that. By the way, did you know he'd fallen for one of his sixth-formers and been suspended for it?'

'Girl or boy?'

'Girl, I think. I never thought to ask, you wicked creature.' She let loose a high laugh that jarred on the stale and sedate office air, bringing Parkes's potato face radiating its grey light once more in their direction. Glenda returned a sharp glare and he pursed his lips minutely, lowering his head again to his desk and the secretary he was instructing at his side. 'How's Mike?'

Glenda was the only human being Susan had ever

known who used the shortened version of her husband's name. How was Michael? A troublesome question at the best of times. Even more so these days, especially after that queer business a week before when he had seemed quite disturbingly odd, brushing her aside so rudely, that peculiar bile that he hid so ruthlessly seeming about to spill for once. Susan wished it would, praying, sometimes, for a new equilibrium in their lives, adjustment to the different path in their relationship which she at least knew was inevitable now. 'He's OK, I suppose. Doesn't have much to say for himself, these days. Moody, you know how he gets. I still want to know who Martin is.'

'Really Susan,' Glenda said, with mock gravity, 'I cannot speak his name aloud.'

'Very well, then . . .'

'However, I can offer a large clue.'

She picked up a memorandum from beneath the pile of papers at Susan's side, pointing a manicured finger at the list of personnel beneath the Jupiter Services (UK) plc letterhead.

Susan gawped in genuine surprise. 'That Martin? The director? Martin . . .'

Glenda playfully pressed her fingers lightly on Susan's lips. 'Please, dearie. Please.'

'My, you have come up in the world.'

'I like to think I'm finding my natural level, that's all. I've gravitated upwards, you might say.' She preened.

Parkes rose in his den and came out into the office, walking ponderously along the nearest of the three desk-bordered aisles. Glenda ignored his approach. 'If you and Mike ever fancy a foursome, you'll find Martin great fun. Good for your career too, if that's what you want,' she said with a wink.

'I'm not sure I'll have much of a career in a moment,' said Susan, nodding towards the supervisor. 'You'll get me kept behind after school.'

Glenda looked at Parkes, now only six feet away, and made a sphincter with her lips. 'Yeah, well, I'll go. Seriously, though, if you ever fancy a bash on the town, M is much generous. And the company's expense account can be so elastic,' she said loudly. 'Come on your own if you think Michael will just sulk.'

'Thanks. I will think about it.'

Glenda – such a presence – breezed away down the aisle. Parkes nodded meanly, a gesture Susan's friend did not acknowledge. He made room for her to pass before he paced softly, this quiet, unsatiated predator, past Susan who smiled to herself and skimmed another wordy proposal from the now less formidable-looking pile at her elbow.

The grey day sank quickly and without trace into a moonless evening as, two hours later, Susan walked along the silvery-lit streets to descend the steps into the tiled warren of the tube station, slightly resenting the way she was always infected by the hurrying wash of peeved-looking commuters, men and women swimming around her in dreadful haste, seeming to hate every second of their time lost in this unnatural place. At moments like this she envied Michael's independence, his freedom from the crowd. She thought about Glenda's suggestion of an evening out and knew that Michael would detest the idea. When they had first met, he would have gone and have professed – lying perhaps – his enjoyment of the outing. Now, with the years passing and their company becoming awkward, their desire for intimacy vanishing, goodness how quickly, Susan was becoming sentimental about the way he used at least to try and please her. If she had suggested such a simple venture in the old days, his response would probably have been swathed in startled laughter, the reply of a nervous, cautious man. But he would have agreed. Then.

I am in my thirty-second year and already nostalgic,

thought Susan Crumly. And for more: the old passion, of course, but other, smaller, detached memories would so often come to mind – the smell of the paper, paints and spirits which used to permeate his old clothes, stain his hands, ever so lightly – she never noticed that now. And the languorous way he would set about odd jobs on the house they could neither of them be bothered with these days. He blamed business, readily, though it was true that she had discovered how he would work all day and half the night to get a job finished on time. Yet he never complained about the nature of his work, nor about the customers who she guessed irritated and worried the pleasure from his life. She had rather admired his dedication then, the way he drew so methodically, carefully, with an inspiration that was far from apparent, steelily controlled. She used to like to see his 'art' and, at first, he did not seem to mind her frequent visits to his studio, though she gradually came to sense his proprietorial attitude towards the place. She would not dream of going there, now, unannounced.

Standing on the platform she noticed, with true disappointment, a new poster – for Polo mints – pressed on to the curve of the opposite wall. Last week one of Michael's own designs, for a brand of wholegrain biscuits, had occupied that small subterranean part of London. She wondered if she should mention it to him. Perhaps not.

Buoyed on to the train by the moving, compressed crowd, she was carried to the far doors, hemmed in by the pressure of bodies in winter coats, an attaché case jammed against her thigh. And still her memory wandered, back to a different time, an ox-bow of time, before all this . . .

This what? Her abortion? *Their* abortion? Such a cold word, cruel, the most clinical of the entire language;

arrest of development, termination – there was no gentle way of describing it.

Before this time, the event of their abiding indifference for each other, was a curve of months, years, when there were, in truth, many artifices to their relationship. In that arc of memory were stored images, not of love or passion she now felt, but of an animal curiosity, a happiness of essential quality. That was a time when Michael had not wanted to control every aspect of their lives, when he had not seemed half as intense as he was now, showing nothing of his dread of the unexpected. Once or twice he had even taken her on surprise trips to Brighton where they had eaten in dowdy cafés, ridden on a ghost train, disapproved of the youths who congregated on the sea-front. Or they might visit his mother in Yorkshire and he would show her the places of his childhood, the countryside around the village, the school that was closed now. He would recall a game of derring-do he had played at the age of nine which had involved walking along a length of guttering at the side of an old air-raid shelter. Children had crowded beneath, egging him on at first, then becoming rather quiet as a central bracket was loosened by his weight. The half-pipe sagged, seeming about to collapse. He did not jump to the side, though. It was perfectly all right, he would say, if you didn't look down. He recalled this occasion, each small detail, with a cool pride that disturbed Susan who sensed the partial revelation of some sinister, aggressive aspect of him that she might not care to see. The term before his act of bravado, he said, a classmate had attempted the same feat, falling, breaking his wrist and knee, leaving a kink in his gait that would never be corrected. He should not have looked down, Michael said sagely.

Susan remembered his mother as a pair of pinprick eyes and a long sharp nose. Her hair was waxy-white, long and caught, always, by a butterfly clip perched high on her head. His father had died when he was young. Michael never mentioned his stepfather beyond saying that he had left his mother some years ago. The mother moved around the cluttered council house, her jaw and fingers maligned by a fine tremor, an inoffensive woman, tired of old age. Michael would often berate her for tiny aspects of the way she ran her life, seeming to select the opportunity to attack quite deliberately. This annoyed Susan.

'You should not speak to her that way.'

'It's the way we are with each other. This is what life is like up here.'

'You act like you were a spoilt child.'

'I was not a spoilt child, not by any stretch of the imagination.'

'She's old. What wrong has she done you? You shouldn't pick on her.'

'I'm not picking on her.'

'Will you be that way with me when I am old?'

And when his mother had died, two years ago, Susan could not find an atom of regret in him, no sorrow, nothing given from that iron-bound heart. She had squeezed his hand in the crematorium and he had irritably shaken it away . . .

'Oh, sugar,' she hissed to a man's navy serge shoulders as the train gathered speed and the name of her station slithered past the window. 'Bother and damnation.'

She got off at the next station, a mile and a half further on, and decided to walk home among the company of joggers, shopgirls and tramps. She made her way under the flyover and past the motorway that spewed cars from the overfed giant that was London. Her feet were sore by the time she reached the street where the curtained windows were luminous in reds, blues, Habitat greens, and the pavement was made apple-white by the streetlights. Home. Then, in the turning to the alley, four doors away from their house, she heard a scuffling of feet. From the darkness came a running shape that took her breath, wheeling in front of her, catching her hip. The child squeaked her apology and ran off in pursuit of her friends. Heart still alive with the shock, Susan paused before the house, picking among the things in her handbag, searching for the key. But before she could put it in the lock Michael swept open the door.

'Here at last!' he said.

TWELVE

'Michael?'

'Yes?'

'If you want something to stare at, put the television on.'

'Great idea.'

He darted towards the set, jabbing his finger at the button then returning to the sofa, reassuming his stiff pose.

'You weren't late this evening,' he remarked quietly, his eyes fixed on the middle distance between him and Sue-Ellen Ewing.

'No. And I wasn't late last night, nor the night before, nor the night before that. The night before that, as I've told you many times, Michael, I missed the stop and had to get off at Turnham. I should be happy if you were now satisfied with that explanation.'

'I was concerned with your lateness, that's all.'

'Well, you shouldn't be. I am a grown woman, perfectly capable of looking after myself.'

She turned the pages of her magazine with an angry flick of her wrist. From between the later pages, slivers of white paper slipped out. She flipped to the middle to find neat empty squares where photographs had been.

'Oh God.'

'Now what?' asked her husband.

'Do we now have magpies in this house?'

'Sorry?'

'You know, magpies. Acquisitive creatures. Legend has it that they steal bright shiny objects, or anything that takes their fancy.'

'I'm afraid I don't understand.'

'Rats, perhaps. Very dextrous ones, I would have thought. With a romantic streak, a penchant for male film stars. Look how neatly this picture has been removed.'

She held up the magazine and looked at him through the window in the page that should have been Kenneth Branagh.

'How strange. You should take it back . . .'

'Michael, what is the meaning of this?'

'I don't know anything about it, I swear.'

She folded the magazine and rested it in her lap, her hands limp, arms heavy.

'I don't believe you.'

THIRTEEN

Michael passed his hand across his ribcage then down his left side, rubbing up and down with his palm. 'It's not a continuous pain, though. It just comes on now and again, sort of radiating along here,' he pointed assuredly with his finger, 'and down here. I would say it was a dull, throbbing kind of pain. It seems to match my pulse.' He sniffed, unable to offer more information.

'How often do you check your own pulse?' asked Dr Hay.

'Every now and then. If something's bothering me. Doesn't everyone know how to check their own pulse these days?'

'Each day?'

'Sometimes.'

'How many times each day? Twice? Four times? Every hour? The truth, please.'

'Surely it's not my heart,' said Michael. 'I'm thirty-seven. Statistically the chances of its being a cardiac problem must be quite slim?'

'Do you smoke?'

'I haven't smoked for a long time. Not since my twenties. My first wife used to and . . .'

'Drink?'

'Occasionally. I'm not terribly fond of it. It makes me too, sort of, well, lighthearted, if that doesn't sound silly. And,' he added quickly, 'it upsets my stomach, which is delicate as you know.'

The ageing practitioner stared soberly at his patient, his glare unpitying, unswerving from its quarry. Michael looked away to his side, at the ceiling, the barred window, the AIDS poster depicting a hypodermic needle and a tombstone, another poster showing the correct way to lift heavy objects. He did not want to speak. He would not have known what to say. Eventually Hay grunted the silence away.

'Michael, I think that deep down you and I both know there is some other reason for your coming here so often. I have done my best to accommodate you, listening patiently to all your many physical preoccupations. Much of what you have said to me I could put down to the hysteria of the times about health, this morbid dread of illness that seems to affect everyone, the idea that we can all live forever. Prolonging one's life has become the ultimate objective for people these days. They're forgetting what they can do with their lives. But with you I sense something more systematic at work. I believe you have a fair bit of common sense, but there is a facet of you that I cannot understand. I had hoped, by now, that you might have realized it for yourself. Couldn't you confide in me, just this once? Tell me, Michael, what's on your mind? What is the matter with you?'

Michael shrugged indifferently. 'I don't follow. Can I see an analyst?'

'A psychoanalyst? Why should you want to see someone like that?'

'I have bad dreams.'

'What happens in those dreams?'

'I'm looking for someone I can't find.'

'Tell me who you are looking for. Your mother?'

'That's corny.'

'Your father? Susan?'

86

'No! Look there's nothing else to say. I've told you what's wrong with me. I keep getting this pain in my chest. It's a new pain. You're a doctor aren't you? Why can't you cure that? I'd probably be all right then.'

'I don't think the pain exists.'

'It does exist! It does!' Michael thudded his fist on the desk.

Later that same day, at his studio, unable to work without the most titanic effort, vaguely attaching some importance to trying to get his business functional again, he sat at his draughtsman's board, hopelessly trying to find some new initiative. Hay had calmly refused to help him any more. The doctor's grey eyes, his impassive voice, had affected Michael badly, imbuing his every thought with painful guilt. At the last, he had pleaded for hospital tests on his heart, his stomach, tangential and hasty requests made in the last defensive moments before the death of the interview he had known would prove fruitless even before he had gone there. He felt ashamed of his actions. Now, feeling numbed, gently crushed by the darkness in his beleaguered mind, he stared at the sheet of paper in front of him.

He had been thinking of Susan again. He was always thinking of Susan. Wherever she was in this crowded city, she held his conscious thoughts. He tormented himself with the image of her in a lover's arms, vainly believing that to do so might exorcize his obsession with her. On the sheet of paper where there should have been a tentative outline of a logo for a fast-food shop was a faint sketch of his wife's face. The phone rang for many minutes. It stopped and rang again. He did not answer it. He paced the floor of his studio, staring out of the window. The sun was low, the air still. So many, many houses. He slept at his desk with his head in his hands. When he woke he tried to force himself to work again, without success. He slept again, for a few minutes, perhaps longer, he didn't really know. When he woke again he noticed many drawings of Susan around the room. He stood and counted them. Fifteen. Some had been abandoned in favour of other ideas, and two had thick, grotesquely heavy features. Gathering them in a rough pile, he put them away in a cupboard, his mind empty now, his hands given to fine, involuntary twitches.

FOURTEEN

November now.

They walked in the park on Sunday afternoons, usually in silence, not touching, and any observer might have guessed easily at their locked passions, the anger and misunderstanding that they hid away from each other. Their slow-moving feet turned frost-chilled leaves on the woolly grass, Michael's breath in staccato white snorts on the nipping air, Susan's in slow long plumes. He smelt the rising vapours of the dormant earth. Susan had a cold.

He counted the days since they had sat in this place and she had, as he saw it, wrought the death knell on their mutual trust with her slight killing confession that echoed now more loudly than ever before, those few words that suggested so much . . .

Ninety-nine days ago.

In the evenings, those interminable dead times, their conversation was forced, as unyielding and profitless as the season. Susan did her best, trying to coax the ugly animal she believed had possession of Michael out into the open. But her energies were failing her. Her sympathy too.

'Sometimes I think you just can't bear being away from me. Yet you won't touch me. Why is that, Michael?'

She did not look up as she spoke, offering these words apathetically, a random plunge into the darkness of their expanding alienation. She squinted at her work, the embroidery of a pair of butterfly-shaped antimacassars for the chesterfield, which she had started two years before then set aside, owing to the tedium of their making. She hated them now, but it was something to do to fill the hours, the endless, empty, silent bloody hours.

Her face has a hazy quality, Michael thought. Like an image from one of my many dreams.

Sometimes he seemed to love and to loathe her simultaneously, to be both enchanted and intensely aggrieved by her every movement, however small. In his moments of fleeting rationality and analysis, he wondered about his insatiable wish to monopolize that which he already owned, this wife who was quite obviously devoted to him, who would do anything, he knew, to restore the equilibrium and happiness they had certainly known before.

His eyes jerked up and down from the book he had been pretending to read for weeks, stealing glances at his golden target, that being, that one, one person, the soul he coveted beyond all reason. He measured her presence with his eyes, quantifying her, deifying each of her features, her eyes, her hair, the tip of her nose, her fingers, her legs demurely crossed, each of these things he saw and credited with an unholy purchase. He wondered at the simplicity of this situation, two people in a room together, demanding nothing from each other, a scene he might marvel over were it not for the malign undertones of which he was so disquietingly aware. She removed her spectacles and snapped a piece of cotton with her white sharp teeth. Michael started in his seat. *She must not see me watching her. She must not know how I feel about her.* But in his heart of hearts, for all his sophistry, he felt she knew something was amiss with him.

'What on earth is the matter with you?'

'Nothing. I'm fine. Really I am,' he replied, smiling too generously, putting the book aside, slightly regretting this last action, not sure if he could get away with picking it up again. 'Would you like a glass of wine?' he asked suddenly, without forethought, his unbidden words almost visible on the air.

Susan rethreaded a needle and replaced her spectacles. She bent low over her work once more. 'A small glass, I suppose. If you're having some, that is.'

'Sure. Right,' he said, bouncing to his feet and diving into the kitchen. He hurriedly pulled a bottle from the cold larder, fumbling with it for what seemed like an age, nicking his thumb on the green foil seal, driving the cork in with the corkscrew. He chose and rechose glasses, spilling pink drops on the yellow, ceramic-tiled worktop as he poured the wine. Soon, quickly as he dared, he was back in the lounge with two fine-stemmed glasses filled to the brim. He placed Susan's on the folding table by the side of her chair. He seated himself back on the sofa, taking one huge gulp that griped his stomach. He sipped then, unable to take his eyes off his wife, feeling he might have cheated himself of time that could have been spent with her, time lost while he had meddled in the kitchen. He watched, more motivated than ever. He feasted, feasted . . .

'Michael, will you please stop staring at me like that,' she said in a girlish voice, her eyes unaverted from the intricate detail of her work.

'I'm sorry.' He drained his glass. 'Would you like some more wine?'

'I haven't touched this yet. You have the rest of the bottle if you want it.'

'Fine. I might.'

He did not move. His fingers squeezed the stem of the glass tightly. Then it snapped.

'For God's sake, Michael . . .' Susan said, drily.

'Stupid. Stupid of me. Look at it though. Made of

nothing, these things.' He tossed the two pieces into the waste-paper basket by the small low sideboard behind the open kitchen door.

Susan closed her eyes for an instant, her lips tight, her hands flat on the three-quarters-realized purple butterfly. She relaxed again and carried on teasing at the thread.

'I've been thinking . . .' she began.

'Yes? What have you been thinking?'

'About a holiday.'

'What? On your own?'

'No,' she sighed. 'No need to panic. I mean for the two of us. I don't see that it could possibly do us any harm. We ought to get away from London for a while. Things are not going very well between us at the moment. We both know that, don't we?'

'I wasn't aware of a problem.'

'Well, you should be,' she clipped, setting the embroidery aside in a heap on her sewing tin, an action that inspired a small gasp from Michael that he had difficulty hiding. 'Look at you. You're like a coiled spring.'

'I'm all right,' he stressed. 'A bit wound up, maybe. I'll admit to that. Don't they say that anxiety neurosis is the norm these days?'

Susan controlled herself, her face set hard in the impassivity she felt instinctively best these days. 'Who knows,' she said, wilfully steering the subject, 'we might even enjoy ourselves.'

'Isn't it a bit cold this time of year? For going away?'

'I hadn't intended a mountain hike.'

'What about your work? What will they say? What about my work?'

'Oh hang bloody work,' she crackled, her patience lost. 'I can easily take a few days off. And you've been saying how quiet things have been for you lately.'

She was angry. He could not bear to let her be angry.

'Right. Marvellous idea. Where shall we go?'

'I thought a long weekend. North, somewhere.'

'Ah, to my homelands.'

'No. Not there. Somewhere else. I'll think of something. And I'll make the arrangements.'

'Great. Can't wait!'

Susan blew her nose and rubbed her dry eyes. 'I think I'm going to bed now. This cold's wearing me out,' she said, contriving nasality in her speech.

'I'm tired too,' said Michael. 'I'll come with you.'

FIFTEEN

'Over there, where the severed heads of criminals might often be impaled, the martyr Henry Bartom was brought to die. Beggars were hired to help carry out the murder – five men in all, whom Bartom asked to join him in prayer, to seek absolution for their part in this sinfulness. They refused, perhaps fearing retribution for displaying their allegiance publicly. The act took place at seven in the morning. The blade used was four feet long and the number of strokes applied by the executioner – to alternate sides of the body of the martyr – was nine. The two halves of the torso were left in the street until nine in the evening. Any questions?'

Susan looked aside at the damp stone flags, the crumbling limestone walls thoughtlessly rendered, patched with red brick. Others on the guide's idiosyncratic tour of this old town seemed, like her, not to have anticipated this or any of the accounts offered of carnage and persecution. The men in bright cagoules looked vacant, the women indifferent or else clutching their arms in the fine morning mist, seeming not to want to appear receptive to the mythologizer's thorough details which were being afforded now with a flourish, points of feudal law intermingled with grotesque descriptions of others who had died in this ancient place.

Michael was standing in the centre of the party, appearing not to listen, his face red and wet with the city dew. A drop formed on the end of his nose. He giggled, his shoulders shaking as if he had suffered a mild electric shock. He looked up into the ivory skies then down at his feet, then directly at the guide, laughing again. Susan squeezed his wrist through his raincoat sleeve.

'You should not find this amusing,' she hissed. 'Michael, you're showing us up.'

But with her first three words Michael had simply let fly a single balloon of laughter that echoed in the old street. 'Why should they worry?' he said loudly. 'They're getting their thrills aren't they? Their little bit of horror before tea at the Copper Kettle restaurant?' He laughed again, the outburst of an anarchic adolescent. There were coughs among the small crowd and a shuffling of feet on the grimy cobbles. The guide paused in his anodyne discourse, his fat man's gaze seeking out the heretic among them, settling accusingly on Michael and Susan. Then he resumed with the Royalist occupation of the town. Susan took Michael's arm and led him away. He followed without prompting, sniggering once, shaking his head.

'Haven't we paid?' he remarked noisily.

'Stop it,' grumbled Susan. 'You're acting very stupidly.'

She worked hard to affect an air of ennui as they strolled away across the wet grass verges and into the narrow streets of the town.

She stifled her anger with Michael, letting it mingle with the residual shame the guide seemed to have gleefully and effectively induced in his streetbound audience. She brooded, by way of diversion, about her own comfortable modern life, her lack of conviction about anything momentous in this world, her avoidance of hardship – dear God, how she had been taught to avoid that. Already Michael seemed to have forgotten the guided tour. Such a rare and unselective traveller. The passing tourists and working natives of this place seemed to draw his immediate attention. He watched them, following with his eyes, his head darting around in scant movements. Perhaps he was still seeking some target for mockery, though he appeared enchanted by the overhanging upper storeys of medieval houses, the tiny shop windows beneath, spotlighted and emblazoned with red, green, and white flashes, pink and blue baubles nestled in feathery white, the commercial promptings of Christmas. He lingered at the windows, staring at the goods inside, moving toys, pine kitchen utensils, furs, shoes, miniature furniture restored with tiny brass fittings, cubes of fat-topped raw meat behind which a butcher in a blue and white apron carved and tossed his wares. He was quiet now, almost smiling. Susan thought how sparely he traded with the world, his innate mistrust of human exchange. And yet, here, in this moment, she sensed the child in him, the infant and his adult anger co-existing, so unhappily. I must try and cope with his moods, she thought. Try and make sense of his complexities.

'Why did you laugh at the story that man was telling us?' she asked. 'Once you were so sensitive about serious things.'

'It's all so false,' he said.

'But that was history. The truth. What made you so flippant about it all?'

'It's not truth. Not told like that. Not spoken by a smug buffoon to a bunch of gawping, twentieth-century people with nothing better to do on a dull morning.' He stopped dead in the street, whirling round in front of her and gripping her shoulders. 'You say you can't understand me. I don't think you understand anything that goes on around you. You take everything at face value. You're so ready to accept other people's ideas of truth. Your thoughts are all secondhand. You get them from those stupid magazines you read.'

Susan winced at his succinct, measured cruelty,

seeing the beginnings of a dry, familiar diatribe about her 'privileged' upbringing. Shoppers milled indifferently around them, pointing in windows, their faces illuminated by the lights, dawdling with bright carrier bags, flowers wrapped in cellophane. Michael let go of her and turned to walk on.

At the corner of a busy street where bodies pressed together waiting for the green man, Susan hung back. The lights changed and the crowd spilled between the barriers, Michael among them. Now she simply lacked the will, knowing that this mood of his might last the rest of the day, that the rancour in his mind, when roused, was impossible to dissipate. How tiresome he had become. How empty, hard and unreal. She could not now understand her reasoning behind this three-day holiday, her belief that their continuous company might change the way things had been going between them. Now she was faced with the prospect of his blunt aggression, his criticism, his worst element. She saw him walking aimlessly on, his head above the crowd, away around the corner of the next street. She turned back, feeling resolute and impish, skipping quickly off along a curved, cobbled, downhill thoroughfare of small offices and houses.

Soon she was in a square where oily youths were gathered around motorbikes, hanging out of the windows of patched-up cars, radios grinding rock music on to the moist air. A squat woman in an open white coat served hot dogs from an old converted caravan. A wolf-whistle secretly thrilled her as she quickened her pace, weaving round shallow puddles, away down a road diagonally opposite. There she paused before an old cinema. Cracks ran down its dirty pink-washed walls like the arterial roads on a map. The gloomy glass portal was capped with a vulgar red and chrome fascia beneath which were dazzling caricature hoardings. The place did not appear to have a name. White plastic letters pressed on a black noticeboard told of the latest offering: *Blue Amour II* supported by *Sisters of Doom Harbour*. How Susan might have liked, just once, to sit through something like that alone; even with Michael. Tonight? No. Of course, Michael would never condescend to anything that might be artless . . .

– In a different world, there were susurrating voices on a far island forest. Lover and mistress prepared to be divided by war.

'Carlton? Carlton . . .'

'Kelly, I have to go.'

'The war can go on without us. It doesn't matter about two tiny people in this great big mess.'

'It matters more than you think. Freedom, America.'

'Since when did you care about America? What will America care about you when you're . . .'

'Don't say it! Kelly, I'll be all right.'

The security in its logic. The voices that filled the great smoky auditorium. The vague morals concurring with those of all who lived in that moment. One knew the ending, of course. She had seen so many. And beside her, smoking, patient, her father. 'Tell me if you're bored, Daddy.'

'I'm not bored. If I was, I wouldn't tell you.'

'Now you're making me feel awful. You only came because I wanted to see it again.'

'I was only teasing. Shush, now. Watch the film.'

Susan opened her eyes wide, absorbing the whole wide panorama, deafened now by the tanks and the booming music, trying to fathom the motives of the Japanese general who never laughed, who only had flint for a heart. And at the climax – the lovers reunited, only for Kelly to die in Carlton's arms as the result of a vile malaria picked up from nursing back to health dozens of doe-eyed jungle infants – Susan reached for Tony's arm, letting her crocodile tears make dark specks on his grey sleeve. See, Father, I can cry. I am a woman too . . .

She shuddered. A wanton and restless ghost. How many more like her, I wonder?

A misshapen sun threatened to show itself from behind the mustering clouds. Susan crossed to an alleyway that led to a shopping mall. Litter was sodden on the wet pavement, newspapers stuffed in flower tubs, people idling under damp-heavy canvas awnings, lank hair above bright anoraks. A new and diffuse light filtered from the sky on to ubiquitous tinsel, paper angels, ragged holly. Susan felt a worrying, rising rhythm in her chest. She stopped in the middle of the street, feeling breathless, nauseous. Then she looked back down the mall, recognizing with relief the deceptive steepness of the road she had just climbed. Still feeling dizzy, she sat down on a bench, quite drained of energy. She examined her wet, kid-shod feet. Might she really be ill? Her cold lingering yet? Her 'spot of trouble' belatedly returning to exact some retribution for her success in having dismissed it so neatly from her mind? Susan Crumly shrugged off all these thoughts and forced the lassitude from herself, deciding she might now try and find Michael. She walked vaguely in the direction of the hotel, trying to think up an excuse for her 'losing' her husband.

Twenty minutes later she was treading the few steps to the revolving doors of the hotel. Inside she found Michael in his shirt sleeves, pacing the shiny parquet lobby floor, wringing his hands and haranguing the male receptionist behind the glass enquiry hatch. 'The police. I insist. Now please. No more prevarications. Do you understand me?' he was saying.

The silver-haired man was leaning forward, framed in the glazed opening like a modern-world, black-tied Gainsborough. 'Sir,' came his steady voice, 'I shall comply with your request. If you would just lower your tone a little. There's really no need for a scene.' He lifted the telephone receiver as Susan stepped lightly into the small drama. 'Here Mr Crumly. Your wife, I believe,' he said, looking at Susan with a glad expression. 'I trust your mind will now be at rest,' he added with a hint of sarcasm as he replaced the receiver.

'Michael? What's going on?'

His eyes seemed fused with lightning, his matted hair swept forward in bootlace strands on his sweat-shiny forehead. He virtually leapt at her, crushing her in his arms. Then he held her away from him. 'Where have you been?' he cried. 'Oh Susan, where did you get to? Tell me.'

'Nowhere. I just lost you in the crowd. Michael, please calm down. I can't see why you're making such a fuss.'

He let his hands drop beside him and shook his head. Minutes later, in their room, he was sitting on the edge of the bed, rubbing his eyes, staring at the space between his feet. 'Let's go home,' he said softly, as if in prayer. 'I hate this place. Why did we come here? It was an awful idea.'

'We came to get away from it all. You're meant to enjoy this sort of thing. Anyway, we've paid until Monday,' Susan replied, knowing her heart was not in this last piece of slender reasoning.

'I don't feel right here. Nothing feels right these days.'

This has the makings of a confession, Susan thought, hopefully.

'I don't know what it is about me. It's just that when you're not there . . .'

'Yes?'

'Well, like this morning. When I'd lost you . . .'

'Go on.'

'I thought you might be lying dead somewhere.'

Susan was unconvinced, but she sat beside him on

100

the bed, cradling him in her arms, stroking a curled snake of hair from his forehead, feeling the dampness in his white crumpled shirt. 'You are a silly,' she said, kissing his fingers, holding his hand against her cheek. 'Is there anything else you want to tell me?'

'I just can't stay here. I can't, I can't . . .'

'All right. Don't take on so.'

She lifted his face and saw the eyelids fluttering, feeling the limpness in his body that he was trying to fight. Soon he might sleep. That, at least, would be something.

SIXTEEN

How Michael wanted her now. How he yearned to possess each hair on her head, coveted her flesh, each sinew and cell of her.

The return to London and familiar surroundings lifted his spirits. Indeed, he began to experience many contradictory sensations – excitement and misery, aberration and rationality, again the feeling that he was on the brink of something momentous. All these tendencies seemed to surge and fall within him, often in the space of a few moments, so that his actions, his reasoning, were not sustained by any one inclination.

Mad. Mad. I must be quite insane.

His abiding and slight insight – uninvited, transitory – informed him that all his anxieties were focused on Susan, on his need for her perpetual presence. And he knew such intensity of feeling was a dangerous thing, and that he should on no account divulge his obsessions to her, sensing, as he did, that secrecy was a bigger part of all this, if only for some semblance of self-preservation.

He wanted to own each moment of her time, to seek the impossible, a place out of time, bound above the hours, the days in which they were imprisoned. If only there were some other target for his attention. If only . . .

If only I knew her lover.

There had to be someone. Such abstractedness could

not so dominate him without some exterior reason. He could not believe all this was of his own devising. Somewhere in his past, at some time, he must have had cause to suspect the presence of another man in Susan's life. And it must have been too awful to contemplate, for his subconscious had sealed the fact away. Some time, some place, in his past . . .

His attempts at work became farcical, though he would still go to the studio for short periods, idling with his paints, doodling with the accounts in his files. The trip away had unnerved him and he clung fearfully to the old routines of his life. Each morning – he could not help himself – he rose at the same time as Susan, his body taut, waiting for the moment of her stirring, leaping in reflex from the bed the second she left the room. He began accompanying her to the station and she seemed very quiet then, resenting his presence, locked in her own reflections – *What thoughts? What thoughts?* He might take her hand as they walked in the wet and windy weather, chattering a nervous soliloquy, stealing furtive glances at her firmly set face, smiling at her, eliciting no smile in response if she happened to catch him watching her. In her leaden voice, she would say, 'Michael, I have to go now,' shaking herself free of his strong grip. If he could not contain himself he might lunge at her hand again, though she began to anticipate this and was always quickly away, her scissor steps carrying her across the busy street to the yawning mouth of the station. He would grieve over her mild vexation, watching the space she had left behind for long minutes, before he made the painful effort of turning away to go to his studio, or perhaps to return home – he never had a definite plan until that moment.

One day she voiced the most minute intimation that she really did prefer to walk to the tube station on her own. 'I do like a little time alone, though it doesn't really matter.' He apologized excessively, many times over several days, stressing endlessly that he would not trouble her again so unnecessarily. Of course she must have time of her own. But the closing of the front door left a residual dread in Michael that he could not tolerate. How he hated that sound. How he hated the silence that followed. He would try and put off that moment, engaging Susan in the most nonsensical conversations, delaying her by drawing her attention to the most trivial and inconsequential details of their everyday life:

'Come into the kitchen a moment.'

'Michael, I have to go.'

'You've another two minutes yet. You don't want to be standing on the platform too long. It's too cold.' *Who knows who might be there with you?*

'What is it you want?'

'I wondered if I should make tea this evening. For us both.'

'If you like.'

'Well, shall we see what there is.'

'You choose, Michael. I must be going.'

'Are you sure?'

'Yes.'

'See you this evening then.'

'I'll be home. Usual time.'

But at other times, such was his awareness of his irrational behaviour, he would usher Susan from the house many minutes before she needed to leave. Soon he opted for a different tactic, a new *modus operandi* that called for frantic activity and some athleticism on his part.

Seconds after she had gone, each weekday morning, Michael would rush from the rear of the house, sprint down the alley and across two traffic-crushed roads to the park where he had found a vantage point from which, if he had been quick enough, he would be able to see, across a hockey pitch and distant shrubbery, his wife passing from the end of the avenue to the station entrance. Then he might run across to where she had been, straining to hear the announcement of the arrival of her train before going to his studio to do nothing of value except count the minutes before he might return to his hiding place, usually an hour before she was due, to await Susan's return.

At five-fifteen, if all was normal, he would catch the glimpse of her that he craved as she started the short journey back to their house. He felt compelled to be there when she arrived, an anxiety that called for fine calculation of the time it took him to make his way back along his secret route. The traffic was at its worst then, and if he had trouble crossing the two roads he could never easily calm himself for the moment when she entered through the front door. If it had been raining and he looked even more dishevelled than usual, he might make weak excuses about just having put rubbish in the alley, or having been to the postbox, the latter invention being elaborately embellished with lies about letters he had written to people she did not know, imaginary clients of his. 'Just what time,' she once asked, with searing penetration, 'do you spend at your studio these days?' He laughed this off, but could not properly answer.

Soon, even this, the trailing back and forth at the extremes of winter daylight hours, was not enough to satisfy him. The darkening December days had a hole in them that was not filled by Susan, and he sought compensation by travelling to town on a later train.

At first he was happy simply to stroll along the wide pavement on the street where she worked, glancing up at the second floor of the tall modern building. In one of the windows he thought he could see her pale green mac hanging on a hat stand next to a filing cabinet at the entrance to the office. Sometimes he might be elevated to ecstasy by seeing her in person, though he had always to turn his face, twist away his familiar thin frame in case she spotted him. He took to hanging around in that street – what else did he have to do? What other facet of his life was endowed with such burning consequence? – sitting in a nearby café from where he could enjoy an uninterrupted view of the wide uncurtained windows that stared over this part of town.

The whole act began to seem like an adventure to Michael. He would wait for hours for her tiny fitful appearances as she stood from the desk he could not see, passing with papers in her hands, lifting box files from high shelves. She might hurt herself, they should not make her do that, he thought. Once, having waited almost three hours to see her, and his concentration having become so intense, his body so tautly poised, when he did at last catch sight of her thick dark hair (now it was much as it used to be), her pretty face in profile and the dreamlike flow of her ponderous move-ments, his breath was taken from him and he shot to his feet, scattering the long-cold cup and saucer across the shiny floor of the quiet eating-house. A waitress, who must have been watching him for days, brought the manager who asked Michael to leave. He went without a word of objection, though he returned the next day and on several subsequent days.

Then he stopped going there at all, for he found a new, more advantageous viewpoint on the staircase of a multi-storey car-park. Although two hundred yards further away now, he could look down into the office and wonder at length about his wife's working activi-ties. *Do you think of me while you are there? Am I in any of your thoughts?*

Passers-by left and sought their cars in the complex, offering only occasional inquisitive glances in the direc-tion of the wraith who stamped his feet, rubbed the damp from his old brown coat, and made copious notes with a stubby pencil in a tattered, spine-scrubbed diary.

Now he had taken to writing down all that he felt might be relevant about Susan's day. For 10 December he entered:

Routine day. P (the office manager) seems absent. Need to know more about this man and about who assumes authority when he is not there. Q? G? X? Surely not Susan? At least today P is not bending over Susan in his over-attentive way. Horseplay at break time. Some telephone activity with seven-minute conversation at 10.35. To whom? What business could take so long? Lunch in the building, somewhere. Looks tired (afternoon). Reason? All work stopped at 3.15 when G (familiar-looking woman – female colleague from another department) brought a boxed cake into the room. A celebration?

And, later in the same entry:

Gently quizzed about P and about who takes control when he is not there. Told it is M who is the token deputy. Can't believe it somehow. Probed tentatively about cake business. Feel uneasy with explanation that it was G's birthday.

So went the pattern of these few weeks. Michael might have felt quite happy with all this, knowing he was imposing some kind of conscious order on his vast preoccupations with his wife, a timetable to structure the endless hours of unrequited longing.

I love her. Simply that.

But in other moments, times of hesitation and displacement, he recognized the bizarre aspects of this love, seeing it in his dreams as a barbed and splintered thing, a fixed reflection in the shards of a broken mirror, cold and bereft of natural desire and affiliation with its object. That much, in bleak hours, he fleetingly understood.

From what rotten part of me does all this come? When, in my existence on this earth, my faulty dealings with the world, could this madness have begun?

SEVENTEEN

When Michael was a boy his father would sometimes take him and his brother Ben to visit their Aunt Dora who had become distracted in her final years. Michael's mother was not inclined to go with them. She said the place, and the people in it, upset her.

Poor Aunt Dora, with her sad moon face and the pee running down her legs. Pitiful.

When they arrived at the hospital Dora had always to be searched for, since she trudged the old ward from the moment of her rising to the time of her being persuaded to return to bed at night. Her stamina was incomprehensible, though if the three male Crumlys went in the evening she might be tiring by then, staggering into furniture and walls, cursing, perhaps resting, but only for a few moments, just long enough to acquire some new whit of energy for the resumption of her wandering. Michael's father, a biddable, patient man, would gently coax his sister to a chair around which he and his two sons would sit. Then he would try and maintain the old lady's poor attention by popping soft sweets in her toothless mouth. But she simply could not keep still for long.

'I have to be going now,' she would suddenly announce.

'Going where, Dora?'

'Why, away home, of course.'

'But Dora, this is your home now. Have you forgotten again?'

'Oh piff. Father will be waiting. He'll be wanting his supper. And he'll have my hide if I'm late. You should be going too. You shouldn't be sitting around here.'

'Dora,' Michael's father would begin for the umpteenth time, 'Father's dead. He died a long time ago. Don't you remember? You and I and Alice and Grace all had to look after ourselves then. You were the one who kept us together. You wouldn't hear of our being parted. Father's simply not here any more. Do try and remember.'

'Rubbish. Get away from me,' the ancient would say, standing, seeing in the corner of her eye her brother's hand extended in another pleading invitation to get her to sit down.

'Can't you stay and talk awhile? Look, Ben's here. And Michael. Do you remember little Michael?'

'I'll go,' she would say, utterly possessed by her great, invisible anxiety. 'It will be dark soon.'

She might pause then, sighing, as if in a minute and passing reflection of her brother's words. She would shrug her shoulders, perhaps wipe her mouth with the back of her hand, looking at the residue on her knuckles.

'I'll say goodbye to you all.'

'Goodbye, Auntie Dora,' Michael and Ben would dutifully chant on prompting from their father.

And she would range away in her stained, floppy slippers, on a circuit of that large cluttered room, into the dormitory, her shoulders slanted with fatigue, tripping in curves about the equidistant metal-framed beds, haranguing the many ghosts that lived in her mind.

Michael's father would smile faintly and sadly at his two sons while they waited for her to reappear. Michael himself would fidget and watch the other old women, his young eyes taken by their childlike disinhibition, the way they pulled at and lifted their clothes, fighting with each other, striking brief sharp blows in passing. He listened to their whining and their laughter and stared at those many more who sat and offered not a word to the world.

Quite unintentionally, Aunt Dora would usually find her way back to them, though she had, of course, completely forgotten their presence by then. Michael's father would greet her anew, as if for the first time that day, and indeed he might be rewarded with a momentary recognition and a warm, cavernous, generous smile that was appropriate to the kind-hearted person Dora used to be. Then they would all sit down together and repeat the earlier conversation over again, perhaps with minor variations, reiterated comments from previous visits about people Dora would have known, about the weather, the coming of Easter, the War, anything that might register with her. Michael, young as he was, knew that his father's efforts were laudable but in vain, born only of a difficult, dour sense of family duty. After a few minutes it was quite obvious that Dora had not the slightest idea who they all were.

When his parents were not around, Michael once cruelly imitated his sad aunt, sauntering about the living-room of their council house, nudging into furniture, his shoulders awry. 'I'll be away home now to fix my old Da some supper. He's waiting, you know. If I'm late he'll fetch the bloody brush to me and give me a real bloody hiding.'

Ben, four years older than Michael and getting lofty in his ways, looked up from the newspaper he was reading and stated that it was wrong to mock those worse off than oneself. 'Anyway, she's not mad.'

'She is, too,' Michael countered vehemently. 'She's crackers. Anyone can see that.'

'No she is not "crackers". Her brain cells are packing up, that's all. That's what makes her forget everything.'

'Home now, to my old pappy . . .'

'You oughtn't do that,' Ben said indignantly. 'It might happen to you one day. Then how would you feel?'

Michael considered this briefly, genuinely appalled by the prospect of his own derangement. He ran outside to continue his mimickry, bouncing off the side wall of the house, trotting around the garden with his arms folded in front of him. He felt very soured by his brother's attitude to what he thought had been a good and witty take-off of their unfortunate relative and her predicament. Then he too quickly saw the wickedness in his actions.

Deflated, he ambled to the end of the garden to sit down on the steps that led up to the side door of their ramshackle garage. He made circles in the dust with his black-plimsolled feet, looking back and squinting up at the starlings on the roof-ridge, measuring the height of the house with his eyes. At an upstairs window he saw the foreground figure of his mother, passive and grey, returning his stare without gesture. Behind her was the vague silhouette of his father who appeared to be making small demonstrative movements with his hands. Another argument, Michael thought. His father left the bedroom, slamming the door, the sound of which came to Michael as a soft thud.

Young as he was, Michael began to understand, with a sense of bewilderment and exclusion, the 'arrangement' between his parents. It might as well have been written on the air, for he saw it in his mother's far-seeing eyes, heard it in his father's dark silence when they returned home, that system of consent whereby, during their long visits to their unhappy aunt, his mother met with her lover, her husband agreeing as long as she did not break up the family. Ben knew and must have been privy to the agreement, but he would not be drawn on the subject.

Aunt Dora's inexorable decline spanned seven years

– Michael could not remember her any other way – and she died a shrivelled thing, babbling in her own mess, needing to be fed mince and mash with a spoon. Though by six months she outlived Michael's father who died of a stroke, falling like a stone one day as he left the factory where he worked . . .

EIGHTEEN

Once upon a time Michael Crumly stood beside a hole in the ground listening to the rise and fall of a priest's fibrous voice, glancing at the man's white hands clasped beneath a Bible. He watched the brown earth teeming down on the wooden chest that held his father. Then he snatched his mother away. He knew only the fact of his father's death, the forms his mother had to fill, the relatives that descended as one on the small house, the numbing void left behind. His mother thought him simply unimpressed, far down the road to the loner she feared he would become, wilfully self-reliant, a heart like a clenched fist. After the funeral, alone with her in the house that had hummed with a sense of relief and, to Michael's mind, a blasphemous celebration of departure, he asked her: 'If you were to die, what would happen to me and Ben?'

She would not answer at first.

'Who would look after us?' he insisted.

'I'm not going to die,' she replied. 'Not for a very long time.'

'But you will one day?'

'Michael, I don't know if this is really the time for such a discussion. You're a little young . . .'

'I'm not too young. I know what's happened. I know why Dad died.'

'Do you now? He had a stroke, a sort of seizure, it's very common. I think we've been through this . . .'

'He died because his heart was all smashed up. You broke it by seeing that other man. Why did you do that to him?'

His mother bowed her head. 'Please, Michael. No more.'

'I want to know. It's only fair that you tell me.'

'When you're older you might understand.'

'I'm old enough now! Tell me, tell me, tell me.'

She hugged his iron-limbed body to her, but he broke free and ran from the house. 'Michael, come back, listen to me . . .'

Seven weeks later, ignoring the frowns and unheard asides of her own and her late husband's family, Michael's mother married Daniel, her lover. She felt new, young and vigorous again, seeking with an appetite all that she felt she had missed with her decade-older first husband. She did not worry about Ben who was maturing quickly and took readily to Dan, perhaps adopting a little too easily his affected air of worldliness, but that did not seem important. Michael, though, would need handling tenderly, appeasing, for as long as it might take for him to come round. She would not think she had ever done a bad thing for she had needed renewal, faith in herself, freedom from the bad decisions of her past, a marriage hastily entered into because of one stupid, stupid mistake. And when she had miscarried that first child, convention, that self-righteous, snarling watchdog of her world, had demanded that the error be compounded, not once (with Ben) but twice. Now, in her forty-third year, she would not be denied her happiness. Stanley, that dour, humble, good man, had gone. She had never loved him. Now she had the chance of a life on her own terms, an opportunity usually only afforded in fairy tales that begin *once upon a time* . . .

She watched how Michael stole short, furtive glances at Dan and she tried to see her new husband from her youngest son's point of view, physically – this compact, earthy newcomer with his fair, untidy hair, this solid, twinkling-eyed man who had taken the place of old Stan, who had been a good father, she had to admit . . .

I will not be denied, the boy must learn the ways of the world. She noted how studiously Michael avoided using his stepfather's name and how shocked he was when he first saw Daniel's clay-caked boots outside the back door when he came home from school. Daniel, home himself from the building-site, was also sensitive to all this and he carefully avoided the armchair that had been Michael's father's, which Michael would seek to occupy himself – picking at his tea on the plate he would balance on his knee, silently chewing as he watched television. And Michael was also distancing himself from Ben as if he secretly loathed the facility with which his brother had adapted to the new situation, to Daniel.

Where are you going in that secret world of yours? Too far, too far. This cannot be my fault. Tell me it isn't. I need to know. I need to be released of this guilt.

Michael steals through the winter night to the brick wash-house behind the house, to gaze through the window at the remote-controlled aircraft Dan and Ben have built together, envious of the crimson, yellow and white livery, the businesslike engine, oily-black and glinting in the shadows. From behind him a voice, a kindness that he dreaded. 'We're taking her up to the moor tomorrow. Maiden flight. Will you come?' asks Daniel.

Now the chance for compromise. Now the opportunity to forget the precipitate thoughts in his head, to become the boy he still could be. But, 'No. Thank you. I don't think so.'

Later . . .

'The kid wants his father back. He wants an impossible thing. I try my best. What more can I do?'

'Nothing. He's being difficult, that's all. He'll come round. He'll have to,' she said, unconvinced by her own words.

The two linked with each other in the cool night light that settled like snow on the objects in their bedroom. Living, living, she thought. I am alive. And she drifted into the thoughtlessness of lovemaking. *Me. I am me. For the first time. Heaven on earth.*

Then she heard Michael's plaintive cries from the next room, the beckoning cry of an old duty that aged her in an instant. She freed herself from Daniel, hot and bedraggled, pulling on her dressing-gown in the cloying darkness.

'Nightmares?' she asked, switching on the light in her son's room.

'I thought I was being buried alive. I saw the earth falling on my face. I couldn't breathe,' he said, his eyes wide and gleaming, his face a stern white. Then he rolled over and cried. She sat on the bed and caressed his head, rubbing the tense muscles in his neck.

'Michael,' she began, as gently as she could, 'this must stop. I want you to give up this behaviour now. Your father has gone and none of this will bring him back. At least try and think how he might have wanted you to get on with your life. Try and remember him for the good man he was. Try and think of him . . .'

'Go away,' he whispered. 'I don't want you. I don't want anyone. You're no use to me.'

She felt a sharp misery. How she willed wisdom to come to him, understanding, forgiveness for the child-ish ways of adults.

You are slipping away from me, and it is all of your own choosing. I have tried to help you. But I will not be denied. Once, in a life that is careless about the likes of me, I was given another chance . . .

'If that's the way you want to play your silly game,' she said, standing. At the door she halted. 'Just how much longer does this go on, Michael? When are you going to stop making everyone else's life so bloody miserable?'

Once upon a time . . .

'Leave me alone.'

NINETEEN

Once upon a time in a young boy's life . . .

So much light up here. Such coolness. How clear the sky – blue, blue, only beautiful blue. And there! Look! The moon, full and bright! A morning moon! Michael gave a little howl of delight and looked from the pale golden disc to the crowd below, the faces like small flowers on the playground tarmac, yet near, only fifteen feet away. A larger body clawed its way through, slowly, its big male face intent on the boy standing there, already preparing to embark on his fearless journey along the guttering that skirted the flat roof of the old air-raid shelter.

'Michael,' called the teacher, 'step to your side. Don't look down. Just step aside and we'll say no more about it.' His voice was quiet, hoarse and appealing. 'Will you do that for me?'

But Michael was gaining confidence, a self-belief to set beside his foolhardiness, a trust that Fate would banish all misgivings. In truth, the gutter was amply wide for his hesistantly probing feet. Eighteen yards from start to finish. When he got to the end, he might just turn around and come back again! He stuck out his elbows for balance. On and on. Not looking down, never looking back. Happy. Almost blissfully so.

'Crumly? Can you hear me?' said the face beneath him, following in some remote part of his consciousness. 'Michael?'

One foot in front of the other in the dry grime of the metal gully. He toed a fledgling sparrow's corpse to the ground and gave a little gasp as he teetered with the effort. Half-way along, a bracket loosed itself from the old soft mortar and the iron path groaned and dipped, becoming elastic beneath him. It would hold though, he was very certain about that. For him alone there was a truth to all this, an assured destiny decided somewhere else at some other time. He wobbled his way to the far end and sat on a column of bricks that had been stacked there to prevent a corrugated portion of the roof being lifted by the wind.

'Michael? Will you come down now, please?'

He sighed, his resolution deserting him, and shinned down a drainpipe. Swift, the headmaster who had watched all this and had been calling to him, dispersed the whispering crowd with a measured glare. The children retreated, murmuring seriously, bewitched by the event, casting backward glances at Michael and old Swifty who put an arm round the boy's shoulder and gestured him away.

In the cool dark study, among the chattels there – drums of powder paint, piles of rubber mats, stepladders, 'The Anatomy Of An Elder Tree' above the fireplace – Michael wept bitterly. Swift seated himself on a red plastic chair opposite the boy, unsure of himself. His old college had told him nothing about situations like this. I need to be understanding, gallant, he thought, without a grain of self-confidence. I have seen this before. It is as if the child wants to be punished. I will not rise to that.

Many minutes passed. Children filed past the closed door, whooping and shouting, on their way to their classrooms. Swift wished the Crumly boy would stop snivelling. At last, awkwardly, he asked:

'Is all this to do with your father?'

Michael made dusty smears on his wet cheeks.

'I don't know. I can't help myself.'

The teacher longed for his classroom.

'Do you want to go home? You might feel better taking the rest of the day off. Would you like that?'

'No.'

At least he won't snivel again. I know enough about snivelling to realize that.

'How are you getting along with your new step-father? Can you tell me his name?'

'He's taken my mother.'

'Taken her where? You mean there's no one at home?'

'No. No,' Michael said angrily, taking rapid, shallow breaths. 'I mean she's different now. I want things the way they were before.'

'Is your stepfather a bad man? Is he cruel to you and your mother?'

'No, no, no, you don't know what I mean,' Michael said, jumping down from the chair and disconsolately trooping off to his classroom.

Swift ran his fingers through his thinning ginger hair and rued, for the first time that day, not having endured with the Navy after the war.

Once upon a time . . .

His limbs shivering, his resolve uncertain, the boy Michael leapt madly in front of an approaching car, then dashed back out of its path. The driver sounded the horn which wailed in an arc of decreasing sound as the car resumed speed and hurried away. Michael crossed the now empty road and hurried away up the hill, anxious to be away from his brother. But Ben caught him easily with long elegant strides.

'You loony! What did you want to do that for?'

Michael hurried on in a canter. Ben grabbed his shoulder and swung him round.

'Stop. Now. I want to talk to you, you fiendish creature.'

'Well, I don't want to talk to you.'

Ben pushed him up against a wall of one of the houses on the road that led to their home. 'Listen to me Michael,' he said, forcefully. 'You're upsetting everyone, don't you realize that? How long are you going to keep this up, can you tell me? Why are you acting like a spoilt brat?'

'I don't know what you're talking about. Let go of me.'

'I've a good mind to give you the thrashing you're asking for. Do you know how upset Mum is about you? Have you no idea what you're doing to her?'

The younger brother felt an ungodly satisfaction when he heard this and stopped pulling away. Did he want to hear more? He remained still, gloating over the small pain he now knew he was causing his mother.

Ben ignored the whooping greetings of a schoolmate who was passing up the other side of the street.

'Look,' he said, contriving a kindly tone in his voice, 'we all miss the old man. We all wish he was still here. But he's gone. Nothing can change that.'

'You don't miss him. You're glad he's gone. So's Mum.'

'How can you say that about us? That's not fair, and you know it isn't, Michael.'

'I don't care. It's really true. She was glad when he died. She couldn't wait to marry that pig. You think I'm too young to know what went on. You kept me in the dark, all of you. Well I do understand what happened. I know it all.'

Ben rolled his eyes to the sky and gripped Michael's neck with his broad strong hand, pulling at the corner of his jacket.

'You're imagining all this. You think too much . . .'

You think too much. You think too much about everything. That's your trouble Michael . . .

'Dan's a good man. Why can't you try to like him?

What has he done to you? He doesn't lay down the law. He doesn't set a finger on either of us. He's a good sort, Danny. We're lucky. Damned lucky. Can't you see that?'

Michael kicked out and wriggled free, red-faced and insistent. 'He's not our father. I wish he'd leave my mother alone. I wish he would die too. I wish I could kill him.'

'Michael,' shouted Ben, but his brother was away, running up the road where heaps of autumn leaves rustled at the kerbside and a small white dog frollicked parallel, yapping, though it could not keep pace with the boy who yelled and thrashed hedges and lampposts with his feet and fists.

I think you are beautiful this way . . .

To survive, with all the wisdom of innocence, Michael stored away the devils in his heart . . . *more beautiful than anyone I have ever known . . .* made subterranean in a cold pocket of forgetfulness the secret child whom the man Michael remained knowing nothing of, though once, fourteen years later . . .

TWENTY

'I have found a golden pathway in my life. I have the faith I've been searching for all my days,' she announced, a dull heat and contemplation in her milk-white face and flaccid posture.

'I don't know what you mean. Why couldn't you have told me about this before?' Michael asked gently, setting down his work folio, the tiredness he had felt throughout the hot day staying his temper.

'Today I have spoken with the Lord. I am saved. He wishes me to follow him and to abide by his teachings.'

'What Lord? Who are you talking about?'

From the bedroom of their tiny Chiswick flat came a cadaverous youth with a blue spot on his shaved head hurriedly pulling his turquoise and white robes about his body. 'Look man,' he said. 'Like we didn't expect you. I'm really sorry about this. It could've been much easier for you if you hadn't come in on us like this.'

'You must find it in your heart to forgive me, Michael. The Spiritual One will bestow understanding, won't you?'

'Yeah, er, that's right,' said the young man before he dived back into the bedroom, returning with a canvas holdall with clothing and personal belongings – some of which belonged to the gaping, disbelieving Michael – spilling from between the bag's zippy lips.

'I am called!' she cried.

'Hey, er, Mike. We'll be in touch. OK?' said the youth, eliciting no reply. 'Let's go,' he said, grabbing the hand of glassy-eyed Angela, Michael's bride of five weeks.

TWENTY-ONE

'Jealousy can be a good thing in a man. Wholesome, in its place. A woman can bloom with a possessive guy. At least she feels wanted,' Glenda remarked miserably. She picked a little chipped varnish from her thumbnail and glared at the green screen in front of her, the unjustified lines of figures, the semi-comprehensible keyboard beneath.

'So Martin's wife played away, too?' said Susan from the adjacent desk.

'Something like that. There were ructions. Talk of her filing for divorce. Oh, and he was so sweet, Susan. Things seemed to be going religiously well. Why does everything have to go wrong when life, for once, becomes so villainously wonderful?'

Susan did not answer. Glenda cursed under her breath.

'How have you been able to stand this place for so long, Sue? Why are you still here? What did you do wrong?'

'I did not', Susan riposted, 'trifle with a senior director, for one thing.'

'It was not a trifling affair, my dear.'

'You'll get used to it. Who knows, if you behave yourself they might allow you to bounce back Upstairs.'

'Please, dear God, lift me from this place. Take me to your high heavenly home. Send me downstairs, even.

To Despatch. Hell can be no more consummate a trial than this office.'

Parkes glided up from behind and silently laid a sheaf of papers in Glenda's tray. She curled her lip.

'Problems?' cooed Parkes in his ashen way.

'None, thank you,' Glenda replied swiftly.

'You need only ask if you are unsure about anything, Mrs Telford. I realize it is some time since you were last down here with us, but our ways are still simple and require only an applied precision. I feel certain the routine will suggest itself to you again soon,' came the measured tones of Parkes, a wooden man, unsentimental, the company's property, even though he resented it, Susan often thought.

'I am sure it will,' said Glenda, affronted, her hands on the edge of her desk, her eyes scanning the aluminium frame of the hung ceiling. Susan saw the quick loathing in her friend in the set of her pale-lipped mouth, the skin that flushed beneath the heavily laid powder on her cheeks. She hates men, she thought. Maybe she would simply rather be a man – a wish she dealt with by throwing herself at them, offering all that she might imagine herself wanting if she were in their position.

'He's wonderful really, our Mr Parkes,' Glenda remarked, arms folded, as the supervisor returned behind his glass screen. 'Been with the firm for nineteen years. Wonder what he thinks when he looks at all these women under his control? Wonder who's his favourite? Who do you suppose he fantasizes about?'

Susan began to realize that perhaps Parkes had been told about Glenda's flirtation with the company director. And that her friend knew, perhaps sensing she might now be considered embarrassing to have on the payroll.

Glenda tapped furiously on her keyboard. 'Anyone

any idea how you sabotage these damned machines?' she said loudly.

'They have spares,' Susan said, more noisily than she had intended, trying to humour and pacify her friend, to deter her from a more damaging outburst. 'The supply is limitless, so I'm told.'

'I should not be surprised,' said Glenda, now scything briskly into her workload, head bowed, eyes concentrating, defeated.

Susan, who was more used to the dreariness of the work, its thought- and limb-deadening repetition, and who had learned both to apply and to distance herself from it, lifted another proposal form for Jupiter Services (UK) plc into her typewriter. Her own effort was artfully designed, economical and calculated. She worked with only an assumed urgency, knowing thoroughly what was required and when, working parallel to the rituals and systems of the office, never quite allowing the job to absorb her. She would gauge the amount of concentration needed for each piece of work very carefully, apportioning only a small section of her mind to the task, leaving the remainder free for daydreaming.

To avoid making too many mistakes – 'Some errors are inevitable, Mrs Crumly,' Parkes would say quite kindly, handing back a red-biro-scored referral – Susan would stoically force herself to recheck her work twice a day, once before lunch and again thirty minutes before closing time. This she believed to be her only real effort throughout the day. For the rest of the time she was not working, she thought, rather she was imitating work, much the way she felt people, including herself, mimicked life. Small movements of her head, prefigured and practised over the years so that watchers, principally Parkes of course, might consider them personal characteristics (or perhaps he was never fooled), allowed her to feign moments of serious thought about her work, giving the opportunity for a glance at the blessed clock, at her colleagues to either side of her and, at decent intervals, out of the window. Twice a day she would loosen the tension in her back by visiting the stationery cupboard at the rear of the office.

For the next fifteen minutes she toiled studiously, with genuine exertion, knowing that Parkes would be casting furtive glances in Glenda's direction for what remained of the day. In a way, she had rather resented her friend's reappearance at the desk next to hers. Glenda threatened the dreaminess, the predictability of life in the office. Susan could easily manipulate Parkes's formal, though slight, application of discipline, and she was conscientiously sympathetic with his reasonable wish for efficiency. But Glenda would never succumb to any of this – she would work against the system, manipulating it for her own ends, making such a nuisance of herself that they would be forced to move her elsewhere or, as they had done in the past, exert pressure on her to resign.

Usually Susan worked in batches of five with the proposals. This time she completed fifteen at once before allowing herself one of her small, subversive breaks. The effort had truly tired her and she arched her back, scratched her spine, stretched her legs under the desk, suddenly bored with the charade. Fearlessly now, resenting her compliance with the office ritual of obeying Parkes's every wish, she stared out of the window at the grey London skyline broken by the thick finger of the Telecom Tower, the nodding heads of swivelling cranes, the columns of sky between the heavy buildings, the offices being lit against the coming December night, the banks and finance houses and shops opposite, and the new multi-storey car-park – where a familiar outline, head and shoulders only, sidled as if in surprise along the balcony wall.

Michael?

She repeated his name twice in her mind. She rubbed her dry eyes and looked back.

It *is* him.

Suddenly she was alert, woken abruptly from her somnolent routine, the whole office alive in her eyes, the backs of the other girls, the maddening tap of keyboards, the soft purr of the ventilation system, the pounding of her heart. She looked at the hated pieces of paper at her side, then stole another glance out of the window. The grey figure was still. She looked at Parkes sitting behind his desk and could not have cared less if he had come from his stupid den to fire her on the spot that very instant. Her face had warmed with embarrassment. She was quite rooted to her chair. Had anyone else seen Michael? Might they see him now? How long could he have been there? Would someone come up to her and say, 'I see you've noticed our resident peeping Tom!' How could she possibly confront Michael with this?

From a few feet away came Glenda's voice. 'It is a well-known point of industrial law that typists and those manacled to VDUs should be allowed to rest every forty-five minutes,' she grumbled defiantly, taking her bag from her desk drawer and standing to leave the room. 'I've been here for two damned hours. I think I'm owed a break.'

Curse her. She's so infernally selfish. I hate you, Susan thought as Glenda rushed away, her thighs rustling in her stupid tight skirt. I could have taken a break myself, she thought. But even in this moment of acute crisis she knew that two empty desks at once in the office was an unthinkable travesty of Parkes's rules. She sat tight, willing Glenda to return, imagining each detail of her, the gaudy wrist bangle jingling as she puffed on the first of her two cigarettes, inhaling viciously, her free hand resting on the gold leaf necklace around her scrawny neck. Susan bent her head low and tried to concentrate her imagination on each of Glenda's cheap adornments, making herself envy them, trying to rid herself of her huge immediate hatred of her friend's complex, fateful existence. She dared once more to look at Michael. A sniper, she thought abstractedly, I can almost make out his ears. Telephones rang, chairs squeaked with exaggerated, unforgivable regularity in her newly heightened awareness.

Then Glenda was back at her side, loud and happy, lamenting and then compromising over some tiny aspect of her work. All the other flat female exchanges gathered momentum in Susan's head. Rising, rising.

'Mrs Crumly? Mrs Crumly?' Parkes's voice hushed in her ear. 'Are you all right? You look perfectly pale.'

'Do I?' she managed to reply. 'A little anaemia. It's troubled me lately,' she lied.

The supervisor smiled. 'This place gets so stuffy at times,' he said, kindly. 'Perhaps you should take a break.'

'Thank you. I will.'

In a moment of complete insanity she wanted to blurt out about Michael, to ask Parkes to get him removed from the balcony for causing a nuisance. She wanted to shout out about Michael's ridiculous behaviour, to scream about his abstractedness. She had to stand, to move away from this.

'Take your time,' said Parkes.

Susan nodded, knowing that his kindness was a sham and was aimed at Glenda for having taken an unofficial respite.

She crossed the office floor, glancing sideways once at Michael who tottered on the balcony, his hands on the ledge as he sidled along in tandem with her passage to the door, the blessed door that was salvation from the sense of her own sheer naked presence. She looked back and saw Parkes smile and give a little wave.

Is he in on this? Are we all going crazy here?

In the windowless, white-lit corridor she felt faint, hungover, her physical resolve truly threatening to desert her. She went to the washroom and rinsed her face and hands with cold water, not daring to confront her reflection in the mirror. When she came out she looked at the inviting staircase at the end of the corridor. Should she run from the building and face Michael now? In this moment of gathering fury? She consciously set aside the impulse and went to the rest room, which was mercifully empty. She sat down on the one comfortable armchair. Who in this building, she carefully wondered, might know her husband? Glenda, of course. Julie, from Upstairs, had been to the wedding. Sarah Hollingworth, damn her, had flirted with him once at a party, three, no four years ago. Who else? Who?

The minutes passed and Susan struggled with her mingled panic and ire. Soon she would have to decide either to go back to her desk or to flee the place, track down Michael, deal now with this calamity that threatened her sanity.

She stood, at last, feeling a strange lightness in her whole body, and returned to the corridor, her floating physical self walking surefootedly back to the office, her mind still undecided, possibly quite bereft of the ability to make decisions. She looked out of the window as soon as she opened the door. Michael – for it was definitely he – was still there.

'Feeling better now?' Parkes asked through the open door of his room.

'Yes. Thank you,' Susan replied, surprised by the evenness in her own voice, astonished that she could use her voice at all.

She returned to her desk and looked up at the office clock. Three-quarters of an hour left before home. She looked down at her keyboard, determined not to start crying. Then, for one last time, she told herself, she glanced back at the darkening sky, the cranes unmoving above the wet exposed clay of the building-site, the glowing office blocks. She saw the blinking red tail-light of a distant aeroplane lifting into the gloomy late afternoon. And on the balcony where her husband had been standing there was now no one to be seen.

TWENTY-TWO

The cold air burning in his chest, Michael sprinted into
the street, almost knocking over old Ellis-Boyd who
was standing admiring his fondly arranged window of
long strands of gold tinsel framed by old pink and blue
lights.

'Hey! Where's the fire?' stuttered the white-aproned
shopkeeper, spinning once to keep his balance as
Michael tore into the alley.

A quarter moon and the high dull glow of all of
London illuminated strewn milk-cartons, vegetable
peelings, pieces of cooked poultry, tissues and cereal
packets protruding from torn black plastic bags
slumped against yard doors. Michael skipped around
the debris, bouncing against the old brick walls that
were the rear borders of the houses in their street.
Trying to clear three heavily stuffed fallen bags, he
caught his foot and sprawled to the ground. A sharp
pain shot through his knee and his hands were scraped.
Despite being winded, he picked himself up immediately, his mind afire with purpose, and carried on along
the dark tunnel beneath the dirty light of the evening.

He knew he had lingered too long after Susan had
left the station. His mind was full of many doubts about
the day. Had she seen him watching her? Where had
she been when she left the office for so long this
afternoon? By the time he had pushed open the back
yard door, hot and hurt, his face moist with sweat, he

knew he was too late. The light was on in the lounge. He could not stop himself, did not dare to take a few moments to think of an excuse that might explain his actions. He went in through the kitchen door.

Susan, still in her thick winter coat, looked down at his torn trouser knee.

'That looks nasty,' she said in a slight tone that seemed lacking in concern. 'How did you do it?'

'I don't know, I . . .'

'You don't know?'

'Let me finish,' Michael said abruptly. 'I stumbled in the alley. It's very dark out there. Something should be done about it. It's dangerous.'

'What were you doing in the alley?'

'I was there, that's all. It's the way I come home. Why all the questions?'

He stalked through the room, not wanting to wait for an answer.

Upstairs he began taking off his trousers, halting, one bare, socked leg on the carpet, to listen for the sounds of Susan moving around downstairs. Silence. He flung the trousers aside and examined the graze on his knee, touching the blood dry with a Kleenex from a box at Susan's side of the bed, folding back the small triangular flap of peeled skin. Then he hurriedly pulled on a fresh pair of trousers and went to the bathroom to wash his mud- and blood-streaked hands. He peered briefly at the pinprick lacerations on his palms before dabbing them with a towel and hurrying back down the stairs.

The room was still icy cold. He brought matches from the kitchen and lit the gas fire. Susan had taken off her coat and was sitting on the sofa, her hands folded in her lap.

'You're quiet,' he said.

'Yes.'

She seemed to him to be in a daze, preoccupied by something.

'You haven't drawn the curtains.'

She shook her head. 'No one can see in from our own back yard. Does it matter?'

'Yes. Of course it matters,' snapped Michael, surprising them both with his irritability. Why should he be irked by so trifling a thing? He stared at the view of the illuminated ragged-brick wall, the trapezium of light cast there. Perhaps this was . . .

A sign to her lover. He, whoever he is, may be out there waiting for this signal. Susan, why are you doing this to me? This, surely, is evidence enough . . .

Struggling almightily with his suspicions, his burning wish to accuse her outright of infidelity, Michael carefully drew the curtains, reaching high so that they met at the top and absorbed every particle of light from the room. The spreading warmth from the fire took his strength and he slumped down on the sofa. The two sat in silence, Michael seething with contradictory, exigent feelings, Susan apparently composed, looking bored . . .

With me? Thinking of how she might get away?

Eventually she said, 'Michael, if I ask you a question, would you promise to give me a truthful answer?'

'I don't know what you mean.'

'I would rather you didn't lie to me. You wouldn't do that, would you?'

'No. Of course not. Why ask such a thing?'

Susan hesitated, sensing some advantage in using a little deceit herself, thinking it might make it less painful for him if he should own up to being where she had seen him that afternoon. She asked, 'Do you remember a friend of mine from the office – the woman who tried to introduce us all that time ago?'

'I don't think I can remember anyone you work with. You tell me so little about what you do all day.'

'But you must remember Glenda Telford? She was at our wedding. We used to go out with her and her husband. He's a teacher . . .'

'I wish you would get to the point,' Michael interrupted, watching all this from some quiet remove in his head. *Now she is going to tell who he is. Now . . .*

'Glenda remembers you.'

'Does she? So?'

'She said she saw you today. She was late for work and she brushed past you in Wells Street, down near the office. She said hello, but you didn't reply. Her description of you seemed very apt. She said you seemed in an awful hurry to get somewhere. Michael,' Susan asked primly, 'were you in that part of town today?'

'I've been working all day. Why should I be near your office? What could I possibly want there?'

'Michael?' she said, her voice wavering. 'Was it you?'

'Ah, Glenda,' he said, with false good humour. 'I remember her now. Wasn't she the one who kept having all those affairs?'

Susan made no gesture of confirmation.

'I haven't seen her for years,' he continued. 'She must have been mistaken. I doubt that either of us would recognize the other now.' He laughed nervously. 'No it was not me.'

Deadlock.

His wife frowned, believing instinctively that she could not pursue the matter, fearing the irretrievable damage that might ensue.

Hours later, his mind still riddled with conflict and suspicion, Michael compounded the matter further by suddenly laughing out loud, saying, 'Old Glenda? Well, well. Fancy her making a mistake like that. Who would have thought it?'

He laughed again, the knuckles white on his clenched fists.

TWENTY-THREE

Shall I spend all my days this way?

He rifled through Susan's wardrobe, inspecting
dresses, feeling the cottons and the polyesters and the
wools with his fingertips, counting the numbers of
buttons that were fastened and those that were not,
plunging his arms into the Ali-Baba linen basket to find
the underwear she had worn the previous day, carefully removing blouses, T-shirts, cardigans and tights
from the drawer in the dressing-table, noticing something odd about the way these things might be folded,
occasionally finding a loose hair which he would place
on a piece of white paper and ponder for a long time,
unable to determine its colour to his own satisfaction,
certain that it could not be his wife's. Her tangential
confrontation had had a deep effect on him, plunging
him into a pernicious depression that would not lift
until nightfall when her quiet presence in the house
soothed his anxiety. He could no longer follow her to
work, and he spent the anguish-ridden hours wandering the streets of their neighbourhood, idling in his
studio where, one day, he stared miserably at a letter
from De Lacy, the discothèque owner, which
demanded the return of the deposit paid and Michael's
reclamation of the 'substandard' paintings he had supplied. Otherwise, Michael would stay alone in the
house, wondering about his 'discoveries' among
Susan's possessions, his irrational fears, his tormenting

belief in his wife's infidelity, this last gruesome fear controlling all his thoughts.

Yet for all that he lusted for her this way, for all that he was sustained and nourished by his obsession with Susan, for all that he felt he loved her, wanted her, needed to possess every part of her, his mind ever filled with images of her girlish round shoulders, the quick small fingers that flew over the housework, smoothed sheets, embroidered, picked fluff from her skirt, despite all this belief of 'desire', he could no longer bear to touch her. He had, he knew, objectified her in an irreversible way. His ruminations continued unabated.

On Christmas Eve he visited his bank and drew out £2,000, confused as to the amount Susan had suggested they might need for the seasonal break. She had implied that they might spend Christmas weekend at her parents' house, but Michael had responded aggressively to this idea, arguing vigorously and at unnecessary length, a confrontation that inspired a new guilt that he attempted to outwit by visiting a small shop near his studio where he bought her a gift of nine dowdy dresses, excitedly explaining to the assistant that they were for a 'middle-aged spinster sister'. The girl looked at him sardonically. He handed over his bundle of notes and asked her to take what she needed. She peeled £570 from the brick-shaped pile.

On Christmas morning he produced his gifts.

'You might have wrapped them,' said Susan, adding curtly, 'They're not my size anyway. You'll have to take them back.' Then she warmed a little. 'I'll come with you. Perhaps I'll be able to find a brighter style.'

'No. I'll manage.'

They passed the nine-day holiday in rarely interrupted silence, scarcely bothering to leave the house that Susan had furnished with only token decorations, not having made the effort to buy a tree. On Christmas morning they quickly tidied away their gifts from each other and from a handful of relatives with a meek sense of embarrassment. Susan would drink in the evenings but Michael would not join her, making vague remarks about the state of his stomach. One morning he found his wife in the kitchen with a drink in her hand. She said, 'I wish it would snow. It never snows at Christmas. I don't ever remember it.'

– On another Christmas morning, twenty-five years ago, the scion of the house had waited patiently at her bedside for stirrings in the other rooms, for her father groaning and complaining about the hour, her mother going to help the visiting grandmother get dressed. Goodness, what an age would pass before the call from downstairs and she could descend to the big bright room with its furry growths of gold and silver, the fat tree floured with white, sparkling with blue, yellow, red baubles, underneath which were the heaps of presents that Susan knew had been stored away in the brick shelter behind the garage. A bike. A blue velvet dress. White satin slippers. A flame-haired doll. In the evening her mother would change into a long soft gown of green or peach. And the doors of the house were locked tight against the cold winds –

Susan remembered and curled the surface of the half-empty glass against her cheek.

On New Year's Eve Michael suggested that since they no longer seemed interested in making love they might move their double bed into the spare room and replace it with singles. Susan shook him with her angry ripostes: 'Why are you doing this to me? Why do you want to hurt me so much? You're destroying everything. Everything. What's happening to you, Michael? Where does this madness end?' He followed her upstairs and stood outside the bedroom door listening to her weeping. He felt she was behaving erratically, out of character. He wanted to tell her to pull herself together, but some flickering common sense told him that would be unwise. Briefly, he saw her as a distant being, a far star in his twilight-shaded life.

January came, unseasonably warm.

A letter from the Inland Revenue meant a visit to his studio. There he looked detachedly through a heap of mail, including a note from De Lacy Enterprises wryly stating that he would find his paintings deposited in the newsagent's yard together with a clumsy threat of legal proceedings about to be undertaken if 'monies owed' were not returned, with interest, forthwith. He read other heated and more eloquent demands concerning undelivered work he simply could not remember. He put the letters in a pile and sat at his desk, sleeping with his head in his hands, dreaming that he was on trial, unable to answer the charges being made against him by a grotesquely wizened judge of indeterminate sex. He opened his eyes, dreaming yet, seeing a black creature flying in through the door, a bird that brought with it an old air, a miasma of the grave. It circled and squealed, seeming small at first, no bigger than a hand. Then it was large, spreading itself and hovering in front of him, taking away the light as if absorbing it through its skin. Michael fancied he caught something of its countenance – cat-like, with a small snout. Small again, it retreated to perch itself on his easel, licking its paws or claws. One eye, large and brown with only the thinnest of white surround, snared him, and the creature stopped its grooming, hovered in the air, then swooped down towards him, a spectral squeal in its throat.

TWENTY-FOUR

'Mmmm. Lovely pinks. An admirer?'

'Aren't they just wonderful?' said Glenda, picking at the stems of her carnations, tossing them one by one into the tall glass vase on her desk. 'Let's just say – ' She paused, sighing winsomely, looking aged. 'Let's just say they're from someone who cares.'

'Not Martin again?' Susan asked.

'Who? I know no Martin. Oh, I think I know who you mean. A squat, flashy type, given to adultery and abuse of his rather overblown corporate standing? Forgotten now, love. I know who really matters in my life. They're from Ted actually. We've made a pact. A new start. No more philandering. There was only ever meant to be him and me. I don't think I've felt so happy since . . .' She looked into the space above her head that held her imagined past. 'Not since the day we married. You can love twice in your life, I've discovered.'

'Do you mean love the same man twice?'

'Yes, yes, yes,' she said impatiently, tossing the last flower like a spear and screwing up the cellophane wrapping.

Susan turned to her work. In the top drawer of her desk lay her letter of resignation from Jupiter Services (UK) plc. She had offered 4 March, four weeks on Friday, as a suitable date. She would post it on her way home.

Now, she knew, she was trusting instinct alone. She had tolerated all the unhappiness she felt a soul should bear in a lifetime. She hated this place with its childish rituals and obedience to infantile rules. And she no longer cared for London. Once it had charmed and drawn her – now she saw its vapidity, the detached and paranoid lives of those who lived here, the noise, the concrete, the metal, the loathing on every street corner. I have decided well, she thought. As for Michael, she would see. When you felt this strong everything sorted itself out, sooner or later.

TWENTY-FIVE

Michael would still await Susan's arrival at the station, though he no longer bothered to conceal himself, standing at the entrance till she appeared with her shallow smile of greeting. She had voiced no exception to his being there, but if she had he would have stopped this activity too.

In the dead infertile weeks of the new year he became physically weak, sleeping for long periods, late into the afternoon. Sometimes he would set off from home with a vague plan in his mind, for work, for finding Susan – just once, just this one time, he would say to himself – but the idea would have evaporated by the time he reached the end of the street. He might wander by the shops, gazing at the window displays, or he might skulk in the amusement arcade near his studio, seduced by its warmth and spotlighted interior, the synthesis of appalling sound making no impression on him as he watched the pale winter faces of those who fed their robotic attention to Invadertron, BurgerBiter, Mars Repulser. Now and again he would go to the studio and toy with his pencils and paints, thinking he might at least try to redecorate the place to sell the unused portion of his lease. Once he put his largest brush to the wall, but within minutes his concentration had failed him. The marks he made there were odd, unrelated, something else. Something else . . .

Otherwise he might hang around in the park, huddled in his heavy coat, watching people passing with no curiosity or imagination for what they might be doing, what lives they might lead, their loves and hates, their problems. He felt aloof from the passing of time, slightly intoxicated by his old sensation of waiting for something to happen, some calamity or great illumination. He felt removed from the common run of things, from other people's lives, Susan's life, this latter now seeming more untouched by his attentions than ever before.

One day the question that had dominated him through all this time slipped from him, almost as if it had no meaning for him:

'Was the child mine?'

'Yes,' Susan said. 'Though I know I could never convince you of that.'

Quietly doomed, he felt he must continue.

'Do you have a lover? I wish to know, Susan.'

'Michael, I have never taken a lover. There is only you. There has only ever been you since the day we met.'

'How can I know that to be true?' he whispered, eyes downcast, his wife's reassuring hand on his shoulder.

'You must believe me.'

'But I can't.'

She is lying. If only she would admit it. Then I might have justification for all this, proof of my own sanity . . .

Susan sighed with a killing delicacy, saying, 'I cannot satisfy you. If you want your suspicions, have them. They are no business of mine. You seem to be seeking to destroy yourself in some way, but you must not include me in your plan of action. Michael, I cannot be made a scapegoat for your obsessions. I have nothing to deny. I have never been unfaithful to you – it's all in your imagination. In fact, I rather think you wish it were true.'

145

'I don't understand.'

'If I say I haven't done anything, then you think I'm being deceitful. If I owned up to something I haven't done, then I would be guilty. It doesn't add up, Michael. Does it?'

No. If you put it that way . . .

On a grey, and morbidly warm mid-February day Michael Crumly leaned against an advertisement hoarding and watched sheepishly for the familiar face among the weary commuters. Bodies passed in angry shoals. He became conscious of the passing of time, never before having been denied his tiny reward of seeing Susan emerge from the gloom of the station. The waves of travellers thinned. He looked down into the white-tiled portal where the ticket inspector yawned, scratching his head, briefly returning Michael's glare from his booth. Michael shuffled up to the barrier and stared down the staircase to the empty square of platform. Now he became more acutely aware of the time. She was nearly an hour late. Had he missed her? Might she have seen him first, looking shabby and wretched, and have decided that this was the moment when she no longer wanted to be associated with him? He could hardly blame her, he thought. He decided he must return to the house. He began running, feeling light and purposeful, scarcely seeming to touch the pavement with his feet, his heart strong and amazingly compliant with this sudden awakening.

Entering through the door he trod on the morning mail that still littered the hall. The house was cold and quiet.

'Susan?'

The silence was an affront, insulting, cruel. He quickly searched the bedrooms and the back yard, deciding, then, to run back to the station along the route Susan would have taken. Once there, he pushed to the front of a small tutting queue at the enquiries window to ask about the trains.

'Every sixteen minutes until seven-thirty,' came the assistant's spiritless reply.

He stood midstream against the dwindling tides of itinerants that issued from each train. Susan was not among them. Three trains and thirty-five minutes later he returned to the house to ring her office, receiving only the bastard tones of an answering machine. He harangued himself bitterly for not having been more vigilant. The crowds of people flowing from the station seemed still alive in his mind. Have you seen her? Is she among you? Why had he not asked those questions? Stupid, stupid man. His anxiety became boundless and he felt as if in the throes of a sudden bereavement. He wanted to break up their home, the fragile and wholly superfluous objects of their shared life – mirrors, tables, the chiming clock, her idiotic, hated thimbles – suddenly taking on a sinister appeal. Frantic now, not thinking how he might control his rage, he ran from room to room, scattering sundry possessions from the dressing-table, bathroom shelves, kitchen cupboards, rushing out to the yard, back to the front door to halt and stare wild-eyed up the shadowy street where the ubiquitous children played, their ghostly forms static in the gloom while they returned his demonic glares. He returned inside and slumped amongst the slight disarray, his head deep in his hands.

Susan came home just before midnight, having about her the air of someone who has become intentionally drunk. Michael looked at her wobbling in the lounge doorway, his head throbbing with the dry mechanical sounds of his long agitation. She threw her arms around him saying that she wanted to take him to their bed to make love. Now, now, she was saying, if we do it now without thinking everything might be all right again, just as it was before. He hated her completely at that moment. He burst from her arms, sending her twisting in a heap on the floor.

'Have you any idea of the pain you cause me?' he growled, his voice wavering as he kneeled over her crouched body, his mouth close to her pretty ear. But his words were not registering with her. She pulled herself up, seemingly ignorant of his presence, and dropped into the armchair, rubbing her eyes and temples, seeming to drift between composure and unconsciousness, her skin uniformly pale.

'At least tell me where you've been?' Michael insisted, his voice firmer and yet circumscribed with a threatening hysteria.

'I've been out with my friend,' Susan mumbled, head back, eyes closed. 'Am I not allowed friends any more? Is this a new rule?'

'Susan . . .'

She stood then, each slow movement to an upright position made with a painstakingly deliberate effort. 'Excuse me, I feel a little unwell.'

She staggered up the stairs losing her shoes on the way. Michael followed, demanding information, lusting for facts about where she had been, her motives for visiting this savage act of betrayal on him. He longed to hear her voice, anything she might say, but in the bathroom she dropped to her knees and was immediately sick in the lavatory bowl. Michael despised her for her indisposition, roughly picking her up by the arm. 'Let go of me, Michael,' she said wrenching herself free of his grip. She leaned over the washbasin to rinse her face and hands. 'Tell me why you did this to me, Susan,' he screeched. 'Why? Can you tell me?'

'Be quiet,' Susan said placidly, evenly, wiping her lips with the back of her hand. 'The neighbours will hear you. Or do you want people to know how you behave towards me?'

'Susan!'

'Oh, stop it. You're sick Michael. Can't you see that? Are yours the actions of a rational man? There's something drastically wrong with you.' She held a towel to her face and saw her reflection in the mirror, the mascara that she had borrowed from Glenda smeared and giving her a comically satanic look. She was past caring about what she might say. 'I've tried to accommodate your excesses, God knows why. I thought maybe you'd come round. We both know we cannot go on like this. Did you ever stop to think how I might have felt when I saw you gawping at me from that stupid balcony?'

'I don't know what you're talking about.'

'You were there, Michael, I know it was you. Everyone in the office must have known you were there. What do you think it does to me when I have to make excuses to the girls saying I can't go out with them after work because you are waiting for me, ready with your tantrums and your madness if I'm one minute late? And I know you go through my things. You need help. And I don't think I'm the one who can offer it.'

He trailed her from the bathroom as she stepped hesitantly across the small landing to the bedroom. When she collapsed face down on the bed he began shaking her hard, trying to communicate with the strength in his arms, his feelings so confused at this point that he was unsure whether or not he might indeed want to make love to her, perhaps for the pain and distress it might cause her. But he did not. Instead he went back downstairs, enveloped in his humiliation, and he paced the floor hugging himself, rocking, cradling his misery throughout the long night.

TWENTY-SIX

'Mutual trust. No funny business. That's something I've always envied about you and Michael,' said Glenda, tugging her coat collar against the funnelled wind on the steps of Jupiter Services (UK) plc. 'You both seem to know exactly where you stand with each other. You're very lucky.' She scanned the chains of slow-moving cars, buses, taxis and wriggling cyclists.

Susan shuddered against the cold, feeling washed out, her mind occupied with the number of days before she finished with the company. The personnel officer had been very accommodating, quite happy to comply with her wish for confidentiality concerning her resignation, accepting a little too readily her lie that her father had offered her a minor administrative post in his company. The usual watery regrets mingled at the end of a trying Friday afternoon, Susan sensing the calculations already being made in the director's mind about the saving they would make by losing a higher grade, long-term employee and offering the post to a YTS girl, or spreading Susan's workload among the other staff, making her job part-time or dispensing with it altogether. Another company worm, she thought about the personnel officer.

'Good of you to offer me a lift home,' she said. 'I don't know what it is about the tube these days. It seems so claustrophobic. I look at the rail, hear the thing coming along the tunnel, see it bursting out of its tight hole and I just freeze. Bloody panic.'

'I doubt that you're the first to be taken that way,' Glenda commiserated. 'I hate them too.'

'Well, I'm still grateful.'

Susan had thought it a plausible excuse. Last week an assumedly disconsolate youth had leapt to his death on the Bakerloo line and, anyway, it seemed quite acceptable that one should have at least one mental aberration these days – even men went in for neurosis in a big way in the modern world, she thought with bitterness. For the last ten days she would use the bus, even though it meant an extra forty minutes' travelling time each way. She would do all that she could to remove the predictability from her life, to deviate from the routine Michael knew only too well, though he seemed disinclined to follow her anywhere now. Again, though, she felt a little evil, a malice in her soul. When she was away from him his obsessions did not seem so threatening. Still she clung to the possibility that this bizarre situation might resolve itself.

She had not told him about her resignation, hoping for a cool, neutral moment when she might gently explain her intention to slip away to her parents' for a while. To think things over, sort out a new future. And he could come too, if he wished. The old Michael would never have agreed to accompany her there – he detested Eileen and Tony. What would the new Michael do? How would he take this? If his behaviour last night had been anything to go by, he might well react calamitously, perhaps take it out on himself. Or her. Maybe I should stop clinging to the past, causing him pain? Do I not really believe, deep inside myself, that the situation is irretrievable? Am I simply being naïve? Should I not steel myself now and call an end to this? For both our sakes?

'Coo-ee! Here you dozy lump.'

Glenda was waving furiously at the bunched vehicles. An old red Allegro stopped at the kerb, halting the traffic behind it. Susan climbed into the front seat beside Ted. The interior smelt of tobacco and the floor was littered with crumbs and sweet wrappers. 'I'm cadging a ride home, hope you don't mind, Ted?'

'Course not.'

'Her car's broken down,' Glenda chirruped from the back.

'Has it?' he asked.

'No. I don't even own a car.'

Ted smiled and eased the car on into the small space his stopping had created. 'It would have been quite a walk for you,' he said. 'Do you still live at the same place?'

'Yes. We've never moved.'

She wondered about the defensiveness of this last automatic response. I am conditioned by the times, she thought. After five years I am expected to have got on in the world, to have gained material self-improvement as a way of demonstrating and giving substance to the modern notion of achievement.

'I was just telling Susan,' Glenda said loudly, 'about what a great bullock-hearted marriage she and Michael have. Love and faith and all that. Knowing you can depend on each other. Just like you and me, now.'

Susan twisted to look seriously at Glenda who made a circle with her thumb and forefinger and pointed at Ted, stifling a laugh. Her husband smiled warmly, reassuring lines forming around the extremes of his mouth. Susan spotted a raised stamp of red beneath the line of his short receding hair. A birthmark? She had not seen him for a long time. Now he had the bearing of an indulgent, overweight man who looked as if he would have made a good father if either of them had ever wanted children. Susan could not imagine him being tough with a class of recalcitrant fifteen-year-olds, especially not those of today who seemed so readily capable of anger and thoughtlessness. At a junction, he leaned over the steering wheel and smartly nipped the car into a narrow, briefly open gap. A blue van sounded its horn, but Ted was unconcerned.

'Aren't you round here somewhere?' Glenda squeaked from behind.

'Yes. Close enough,' she said, though they were yet half a mile from her home.

The High Street. She automatically glanced up at the windows of Michael's studio. There was no light on, but his door was wide open. Would he be in there? Asleep perhaps? Now? Now? Shall I tell him of my plans now? When would she get another opportunity to face him on neutral ground? How often did he leave the house these days? Has fate given me this occasion? Think woman. Think.

'Stop. Stop here.'

'Are you sure?' Ted asked. 'I thought your street was away over towards the river.'

'This is fine, really. I thought I might do a little late shopping.' With what facility all this lying came to her these days.

'If you're absolutely certain.'

'I am.'

Ted slowed the car at the end of the street and Susan got out. She waved at Glenda who smiled broadly and tapped her fingertips on the rear window. Then she walked slowly, gathering the loose belt of her coat around her. Late shoppers dawdled in the lights cast by closing shops. A glassy skin of ice was forming on the crescent-shaped dark puddles on the pavement. A grocer carried half-empty crates of greens into his shop while his gangling assistant, muffled in scarf and overalls, manipulated a pole to push back the window awning.

Susan tried to inspirit herself with some necessary anxiety and a sense of urgency. She could no longer accept Michael's excesses. Last night, when she had come home late, he had seemed on the verge of real violence and it had frightened her. This could not go on. One day I will die she thought, maybe sooner than I think. Only then will I have achieved the wisdom I should have now, at this moment in my life. What might be my death-bed regret if I fail in the next few minutes to sever the dead limb of our marriage?

She lingered in the street, angry with herself for her hesitancy, her poverty of resolve. Glenda would not have been so cautious. She would have stormed up there with her much-practised fury and dealt with the matter as simply as if she were returning an ill-fitting cardigan. But then Glenda would never have tolerated being spied on, having her clothes rummaged through, subjected to endless, thinly veiled interrogations, to tantrums, impotence.

Time, thought Susan, I need time. I could do with a trigger, a catalyst to enliven my slow anger. She paused before the door that led to the unlit staircase, then proceeded to climb, vaguely deciding to accept what the moment afforded, succumbing to a clearer wish for spontaneity and all the resolutions that might bring.

She had not been there for years. There might be much that reminded her of the past, but it would not deter her – there would be a time for reflection later, time alone for the apportioning of blame, guilt. She climbed the stairs slowly, guided only by the weak reflected street-light from the doorway behind.

At first, in the gloom of the place, she thought the studio might have been broken into. Then she thought, with a stab of fear, her eyes growing used to the poor light, that there was a shadowy figure wedged in the corner. Artists' brushes and paper littered the place. There was a smell of damp, of powder and decay. She felt the moisture-streaked wall for the light switch and on finding it saw herself many times over, in savage reds, luminescent greens, black, white, on easels, on canvases leaning against the wall, on curling sheets of paper scattered about the floor beneath her feet, taped to worktops and cupboard doors. And in massive relief, on each of the walls, in every available corner, were more dreadful, fantastic likenesses of her. In some her eyes were empty circles, in others this feature had been made huge and exaggerated. Above the door she saw herself reclining. Sleeping? Dying? To the left of where she was standing, on the biggest expanse of available wall, the crazed artist had painted an enormous face, its mouth open and distorted, caught as if responding to an unimaginable depravity.

Susan wrung her hands tightly about the strap of her bag. How could she have so underestimated the extent of Michael's madness? She struggled to comprehend the significance of the flames of colour before her, the screaming images, thinking to take in as much as she dared, as quickly as possible. She turned over a heap of pencil drawings on his desk and they slithered to the floor, the slight hush of paper caressing paper, the movement, startling her into abject fear. She ran back through the door and on the dark landing turned her face to the wall and cried softly.

Arms encircled her. Strong, muscular. Warm breath on her neck. She screamed.

TWENTY-SEVEN

'You *are* in a poor way. Come on, nothing can be that bad.'

Susan loosed herself from the clutching arms and turned to face Ted who stepped back and placed his hands lightly on her shoulders.

'Oh Ted . . .'

'Glenda was worried. She said you hadn't been yourself for a long time. She was right, wasn't she?' he said. He smiled, dropped his hands and looked through the open door of the studio, craning his neck like an inquisitive kitten. 'Isn't this Michael's place?'

'Don't go in there, please,' Susan beseeched hoarsely, catching him by the hook of his arm. 'I'd like to go now, if you don't mind.'

But Ted pulled himself away from her and went through the door. Susan heard his faint boyish whistle. 'This must be the work of a lunatic,' his voice echoed in the interior. 'Look at this lot. Wow. Say, are these pictures meant to be . . .'

'Please, Ted. I have to go,' Susan called from the landing. 'Take me away from here. Anywhere. I'm begging you.'

She listened to his footsteps as he moved around inspecting the room, short interrupted paces as he went from one ghastly impression to another. When he re-emerged, switching off the light, his brief, almost wry glance chilled Susan's bones. 'We'd better go, then,' he said, gravely, leading the way, trotting quickly down the stairs with Susan trailing in his wake.

Back in the car she felt as cold as a winter grave, thinking that no warmth would ever penetrate to her blood again. She could not bring herself to answer Ted's polite questions. He skirted around the subject of Michael's estrangement, realizing his probing was clumsy, divining the seriousness of the circumstances and dropping the subject altogether.

'I cannot go home,' she said. 'I simply can't.'

'I think I can understand that,' he said.

He drove on through the thinning night traffic, chattering nervously about the school where he taught, the kids, his colleagues, seeming to have to talk about anything to fill the silence. Glenda, he explained, had been called away the moment they had arrived home – some special project to do with her work. Susan knew that this would be a lie.

Soon they had arrived at his and Glenda's house, a place Susan had never been to before and which was not far removed from the home of her imagining: a small, untidy-looking semi-detached on a link road that rose to distant traffic lights and a typically insular suburban community. He swept the car into the short, weedstrewn drive, the lights picking out the first pow-dering of frost on the little rough lawn beneath the bay window. Susan jumped out quickly, standing at the front door, shivering as Ted fumbled among his things on the back seat. Once inside he immediately poured two large brandies, offering one to Susan who accepted the glass and nestled it between her palms, sipping, recoiling slightly from the drink's pungent vapours. She set down the glass and took off her coat.

'I must say,' Ted remarked, 'you do look as if you've had a hard time of things lately.'

'Do I?' she responded dully as she sat back on the low soft settee, her unexpected host sitting on the edge of a shabby armchair. 'The ageing process, perhaps. I don't know what to say. It's all so muddled. I don't understand anything any more.' She feared she was going to cry again. She wanted to cry, to bring back the warmth.

'Want to talk about Michael?'

'I'm not sure that I do.'

'It might help. You can't lock something like that away forever.'

Susan smiled wanly. 'I suppose I do owe you some sort of an explanation. The truth is, well, he's had a kind of fixation about me . . .'

'Is he jealous or something?'

'Sort of, well, more possessive than anything. Sickly possessive. I don't know how long it's been going on. It's not as if it was a physical illness, something you could see. Sometimes I think it's nothing and I forget all about it. It's not easy to think of it as a real, existing thing . . .'

'I'll bet,' said Ted, sipping his brandy.

Susan felt an unavoidable sense of resignation. 'It's all in Michael's mind and I don't know how it will ever go away. I feel guilty sometimes – I feel I may have caused it, yet I don't see how I could have.' She drank the last of her brandy and set the glass down, rubbing her eyes, making an unconvincing show of tiredness. 'I'm frightened, Ted. I've always felt I could cope until recently. It gets worse . . .'

'I don't see how you can possibly blame yourself. Has he seen a doctor? Does he actually realize something's the matter with him?'

She felt the weight of the last few months pressing down on her. She could not bear to look at Ted, her audience, her witness and jury, yet she was grateful for his presence, his abiding *normality* close to her, so close. 'Sometimes,' she said, 'I think Michael knows he's wrestling with a demon, something that's invaded him and won't leave him alone. I don't know if he will ever win the fight. It seems impossible now. I don't know . . .' She halted, sensing the too-familiar prickly warmth in her eyes.

'There's no need to go on, if it upsets you.'

Susan began again, knowing she must push all this outside herself in some way. 'I felt something was wrong . . . oh, I don't know when. He's always been a bit of a loner, though I rather liked him for that. More than that, I loved him. Still could . . .'

For the next two hours she confessed each detail of Michael's obsession as she saw it, the unwanted pregnancy, his unsatiated questioning, his appearance on the balcony, the rest. Her plain voice and Ted's occasional attentive interjection were the only sounds in the small scruffy room. Then, at ten-thirty, the telephone made them both start. Michael?

She listened to Ted's low voice in the hall, his casual and easy tone, and realized that he was not talking to Michael but to someone he knew well. When he returned he repeated Glenda's new deception: 'Well, well. What a busy working life Glenda does lead these days. It seems her business has delayed her and that she must stay the night.'

Later, Susan remembered the lack of regret or suspicion in Ted's voice, sensing that all this might have been an elaborate contrivance on both his and Glenda's part, that, rather than being with Martin, as Susan had first thought, Glenda might be lying awake in some hotel room alone, or she might be at a girlfriend's, while Ted made the slight intimation that he and Susan should spend the night together.

This she thought again as she lay in the musty air of the bedroom in the dim wash of darkness, her stomach burning, burning, feeling the warmth returning to her, inside her, sheepishly remembering the forgotten oblivion of coupling body with body, limb with limb, the release in physical compliance. She drifted off into short, refreshing spells of sleep, waking again and again, disturbed by her lover's snores and grunts which came as if sleep brought him some difficult illness.

In the morning she could smell toasting bread, hear the radio downstairs, and Ted's gentle, contented humming. She felt she had never before been able to think so clearly. She rose and dressed in her workclothes of the day before, knowing she would not be going back to the office today, that she could easily – though it was against her conscience – skip the last few days she had intended to serve there.

'Have you thought what you're going to do?' Ted asked when Susan had joined him at the tiny breakfast table.

She thought he looked very grey and aged in the morning light, a failed husband, a man plucking at time, taking small pieces of it for himself, knowing the gathering speed of its passage. 'Yes. Though I might need your help. Can you help? Need Glenda know?'

'She won't mind. She'll probably think it all rather jolly. That's the way things are with us. You must have realized that by now.' Despite his smile he looked crumpled and defeated and Susan was alerted by the sharp pang of sorrow she felt for him.

'Ted, I'm sorry. You must think I'm using you.'

'Don't think about it,' he said, leaning across the table, kissing her forehead lightly. 'I take it you're going to leave Michael?'

'I must.'

'Will he know? I mean, have you ever intimated as much to him?'

'In the nature of things, I doubt that it was a decision we could ever have reached together.'

'You're quite sure about what you want to do?'

'Quite sure.'

TWENTY-EIGHT

The children in their little kingdom of the street were more vociferous than ever, seeming to taunt Michael with their cries and shrieking laughter. Yet this time he had accepted Susan's failure to return home with an almost propitious understanding, an odd sense of relief. At eleven he had taken himself up to the cold bedroom to sleep, to dream of a year of jumbled seasons, of a life that passed without hardship or conflict, all its minute and ambiguous events turning with an overt perfection, flowing quintessentially, time out, free of discord.

He woke at his once-customary early hour, unwilling to leave the bed and the aftermath of his dreams. He listened to the street waking itself and he was enchanted by its familiarity, the adult voices, the tinkle of the bell on the door of Ellis-Boyd's store and the smooth hum of a world gently intent on a day of industry. He had no idea of the time. Sleep came and went through the day as the world he imagined outside mingled in odd shapes and guises with his dreams. He guessed it was late afternoon when he woke, dry-mouthed and feeble, to hear Susan's wholly unexpected arrival through the front door. He heard her slow, light tread on the staircase and feared it as if it might have been that of an unknown intruder. Then she was in the room, a slight, meddlesome presence, an irritating butterfly, fragile and unwanted. She was talking then, and though none of her first words meant anything to him, he felt that velveteen voice echo in his blood. Between them now lay all the accumulated passions and revulsions of their years together, come full circle. It was as if they were meeting for the first time, each suspicious of the other, trying to guess the other's thoughts, harboured in their individual central selves, each knowing the other less than ever before. 'I think,' Susan was saying, wringing her hands, 'in fact I think I know, deep inside, that somehow – don't ask me how – this is what you have been wanting me to do for some time.'

Michael sat up and threw his legs over the side of the bed, throwing the sheets aside so that his wife might see his nakedness. He scratched his head and grinned. 'You've been with another man.'

Susan struggled with her apprehension and her wish for dignity. 'Does that satisfy you now?' she asked, her voice dry and brittle. 'Tell me Michael, isn't this what you expected from me? Didn't you really force me into this?'

'I suppose this is the end of the road for us?'

'I think it wisest, don't you?'

Michael laughed hollowly; then in a rage he rose and ripped to shreds each item of bedclothing. Susan was screaming at him to stop. He heard her voice come as if from a great distance, perhaps from deep inside himself, and its raucous pitch plucked at some deeply embedded nerve. She was a scratchy, annoying thing in the world of his fury, and he threw his hand out and caught her heavily on her head . . .

See the frail thing tumble . . .

She caught her head on the corner of the dressing-table and whimpered strangely before closing her eyes, a sixpence of blood appearing in her ear.

Michael picked up his clothes and rushed from the room, stepping over his wife's still, prostrate form, unable, even as he caught her shoulder with his toe, to contemplate her presence and what had gone on in the last ninety seconds.

In the rear lounge he dressed and tried to steady himself, but the house, all that he could remember of his life there with Susan, began impinging remorselessly on his mind, the voices of a million conversations, their fears and aspirations, the real love he had experienced with her before all this. He felt hounded by all these devils, and he could not bear it.

He ran from the house and went on running, as fast as he could, seeking exhaustion, obliteration through physical effort, spurred on by a new bizarre kind of joy he could not explain to himself, whooping aloud in the dark early evening. When he could run no more, when the blood that fed his heart and his eyes and his sinuses seemed to be on fire, he wandered without thought into a riverside pub, seduced by its bright lights. There he drank lager and scotch, poisons, he thought, that he had not touched for years. He left half-filled and untouched glasses before the eyes of unamused bartenders in striped shirts and bow ties before moving on to another, undetermined place where he lingered in the crowd standing at the bar before losing his slender patience and leaving. The drink had done nothing to dull the brilliant, searing sense of relief he was feeling inside himself.

He ran on again, through unknown terraced streets where large packed households argued with each other and played loud rock music to heat their differences. He passed down the avenues of the rich and by an industrial estate where alsatian dogs howled at the locked mesh gates. He sauntered then, near to fainting, down a half-lit arcade where vagrants cursed and exchanged slurred incongruous congratulations, and junkies congregated, mirror-eyed, in the company of hard young men Michael did not fear.

Then his surroundings began to look familiar to him, streets he knew, the London he despised, this endless place where he had so foolishly displaced himself so many years ago. Now he strolled with the air of the nonchalant tourist into a road he knew very well, vaguely wondering what instinct might have brought him here.

He pushed open his studio door, casually entering to climb the bare wooden staircase he knew better than himself, the creak of each step bringing the past crashing down, the old smells of damp, of paper and dried paint. He did not bother with the light, preferring to feel his way around instinctively in the gloom.

For a long time he stood in the centre of the room, sensing the return of all the old phantoms that occupied his wretched mind: his family, his first wife, his old employers, his heinous clients, Susan's parents, Susan herself, this whole small world claiming him, spinning in his head. The grotesque paintings on the walls were intermittently illuminated by the lights of cars passing beneath the windows. A quarter moon had risen high and sharp above the purple slated roofs opposite. He tried to remember the words of a nursery rhyme about sliding down the crescent of such a moon, but nothing came to mind. He shuffled his feet and heard the paper rustling on the floor, sheet after sheet strewn like sections of fallen wallpaper.

Moving slowly and deliberately, he went to the shelf beneath the sink and, probing with his fingers in the dark recess, found the large, two-thirds full bottle of clear spirit. He removed the cap and dashed the thin liquid on the floor, against the walls, thinking of each of his old enemies. Then he threw the bottle aside and stumbled over to his desk, from the drawer of which he produced an old box of matches. He laid the spitting yellow flame to the corner of the nearest drawing then sat down in his chair to watch the new dancing light grow over many minutes, the flame being hesitant and choosy over the direction it wanted to take. Soon, though, the smoke was dark on the flickering ceiling, then it was everywhere, in layers of black and periwinkle blue.

TWENTY-NINE

Roland De Lacy, discothèque owner, in his sienna sheepskin coat and scarlet roll-neck sweater, said he would melt if he didn't get out of the hot July sun. He said the heat must be the result of the ozone layer breaking down, then he said he couldn't give a damn about what caused it. He kicked at the litter and the dust on the pavement outside Toddy Wallender's newsagent's shop, bemoaning his miserable fortune of late. 'Now this. I wondered why I never heard from him. Crazy man. Fucking crazy man. Why did I come here?'

Wallender, in his shirt sleeves, standing outside his empty shop, sniffed and patted his small moustache. 'You said on the phone you wanted to see for yourself.'

'How do I get my money back now?' De Lacy whined.

'Search me. You're not the only one owed.'

'He must have been very mad. Did you know him well?'

'He was all right. Minded his own most of the time. Yeah, he was OK.'

'And you? How'd you fare out of this damned mess?'

The two of them looked up at the cat's cradle of blackened and splintered joists that had been the roof and which had been newly exposed by builders. 'Not so good.'

'Insurance OK?'

'So, so. But it doesn't cover you. I'd have preferred it

if he'd made a proper job of it. The insurers say it'll be cheaper to rebuild. I'd rather have had the money – business was lousy, had been for a long time.'

'Hah. So none of us wins?' De Lacy chortled.

'Suppose not,' Wallender said, grinning with him.

'Say, you look like a man who could do with some cheering up. You look like you know how to enjoy yourself. You like to dance? A little boogie with your girl?' He wriggled his fat backside, his arms reaching for the scorching sun.

'I don't mind.'

'A classy dinner? Live music?'

'S'pose.'

'I will send you some complimentary tickets for my disco and you will be my guests and have a bloody good time. Yes?'

'Sounds all right.'

De Lacy slapped him on the shoulder. 'Maybe if you could get your insurance company to cough up the dough instead, you might take a liking to my place. Ever fancy running a disco?'

'No,' Wallender said, after a few moments' thought. 'Not really.'

'Wise man!' De Lacy said, punching him playfully. 'Bloody business stinks. I have taken a shine to you. We are friends. Yes?'

Wallender shrugged and smiled. 'If you like.'

'I do bloody well like. I do. We businessmen must stick together. Who knows when we might come across hard times,' he said, waving a portly finger at the black-webbed roof above.

'Yeah. Who knows?'

THIRTY

'Ten-fifteen in the morning,' announced Eileen Thorpe, licking syrup from the fleshy pads of her palms, 'is as appropriate a time as any for a meal. You should only eat when you are hungry, it's the most obvious logic.' She ladled the treacle on to a slithery pancake. 'And I'm ravenous now. My body tells me this simple truth.' She lifted the plate, slipped the *Daily Telegraph* under her arm and went through to the lounge. A film of rain bristled against the french windows and scuffed the surfaces of the puddles on the cream and pink patio flagstones. 'Bloody weather,' she said. 'Bloody England. One thing I would say about Tony, he did insist on plenty of holidays. Even took me with him sometimes.' She curled her mouth in a wry expression, letting the newspaper fall from beneath her arm before sitting down in front of the television set. She scooped a forkful of the steaming yellow pancake between her lips, chewing reflectively, before setting the plate aside.

'I have to say, I do sometimes wish the bugger was still here. It's alarming the way you can get used to people, even those you despise. If you endure long enough with someone, love and hate seem to become one and the same thing, matters of indifference, inconsequential things. I wonder if his lady mineralogist – God, they call her Daphne, such a stupid name, quite typical of a female scientist, don't you think? – I wonder if frump Daphne waits until he's gone to work to put the washing machine on? He used to hate the sound of that thing, even though you can hardly hear it outside the kitchen – but then that's where he used to take his furtive little phone calls. Sometimes I'd put it on at eleven at night, with nothing inside it, just to rattle him. That scrappy little flat will be full of noises. He'll soon get bored with it. I wonder if they have a woman "to do"? If he came back, I bet he'd ask me if I minded first. Or maybe he'd just chuck his suitcase under the stairs and go up and shower, expecting his supper as if nothing had happened in the last six months.' She picked up her plate again and rolled a dripping ochre lump round the prongs of her fork. 'What say you, poppet?'

'I'm not sure what to think. You've asked me this dozens of times,' said Susan.

'Oh, have I?'

'If you're really pressing me for an opinion . . .'

'Yes?'

'I think he will come back one day. You're, well, sort of static. You don't change for anyone. He always knew where he stood with you, all those years.'

'Mmmm. And will he not know where he "stands" with the tubby Ms Scientist?'

'Have you seen her? You've never mentioned that before.'

'She has long dry straw-coloured hair, enormous lips, wire-rimmed spectacles, of course, and she wears long crimplene frocks with wide plastic belts. I saw her twice. I do have friends of my own, allies, if you like. I was told where they met – a perfectly seedy vegetarian restaurant across town.'

'So you spied on him?'

'Of course, my dear. Wouldn't you?'

'I don't know,' Susan answered.

'He can't possibly stay with her. He may be seventeen years older than her, but her values will be very old-fashioned compared to his. One whiff of his way-wardness and she'll have him out with yesterday's milk bottles.' She took the last skein of pancake on her fork. 'Before he went I warned him not to let her take money from him. He's so foolish with the stuff. You wouldn't think he had the wherewithal to build an empire worth three and a half million, he's such a soft touch.' She put the empty plate aside and looked out at the rain. 'God, I'm so bloody bored these days. I shall have to invent some new interest in my life. Will you be going to see Michael this afternoon?'

'Yes. I think I should. Would you like to come with me?'

Eileen stifled a little wind and thought for a few seconds. 'Probably not, I think. He seems to get so upset when he sees you and I can't bear people who succumb to their emotions.'

'Maybe you see something of yourself in them and that's what concerns you.'

'That's a rather *passé* piece of psychology these days, darling.'

Susan yawned and stretched, leaning back into the comfortable corner of the sofa. 'I don't believe it's me that upsets him. I don't know what it is. I doubt that he really thinks about me these days.' She wriggled her fingers and her bare toes in another stretch. 'I should really consider getting dressed. A bath first, perhaps.'

'And why not?' Eileen said, throwing her arms wide in an unfounded, extravagant gesture of alacrity. She smiled and offered her daughter one of her rare, con-centrated looks. 'It is so nice having you home again, Sue. I should have gone rather potty, I think, if I'd been here alone.'

Half an hour later, in the steam of the upstairs bathroom, Susan rubbed a circle in the wall mirror and looked at her face. It is a younger face these days, she thought. The light in here is very kind to it, though – it makes my features softer. I have a protected look. Now might I accept and nurture the child in me? The new child I might allow to be vulnerable, excitable, undisciplined? Such assumptions I made about 'adulthood'. Heavens, how peaceful life is here. I should never have left – the world outside has little to offer the likes of me, a yet-young woman with such doe-eyed gentle features.

With the tip of her index finger she smoothed the little scar on her left temple. The tender pinkness had almost gone, just a hairline remaining at the root. The rest of it was turning brown which she did not really mind since it could never be thought of as ugly.

Almost a year had passed since that moment, in that other time, when Michael had struck out at her, a blow which had caused no pain and was sinister only in its unexpectedness. She had woken within moments, if, indeed, she had ever been unconscious at all. The dark petals of blood on the stone-coloured carpet had worried her though. Ted had been so good, coming into the house when he had seen Michael running away, taking her back to his home, calling the doctor whose suggestions Susan had quickly rejected, knowing that she could never spend another night in the hospital where she had forfeited parenthood.

Michael, when they had lifted him from his smoke-filled staircase, had been taken to another place. His hands and face had been scorched by the heat, but there had been no scarring for him. His appearance on the stairs suggested that he might have rescinded at the last minute any idea he had had of killing himself – anyone else would have been well away before the flames took hold. He would never be the same again, they said. It was the smoke that had damaged him. Susan often wondered if this were true.

After her bath she spent an hour dressing, watching the rain depart from the skies above Peterborough.

Then she joined her mother for a salad lunch and ordered a taxi.

She would not stay long today, she thought. Later she might walk into the town to the new store she and Eileen had visited the Saturday before – both of them had deeply admired a pair of sapphire and gold earrings, and the silk blouses were very elegant. She paid the driver and made her way through the gardens of the home her father had strongly insisted on paying for, to give Michael the very best of care.

On the old cottage ward the nurse brought Susan's husband to the small visiting room, leading him by the hand and seating him beside his wife. 'You look well today, Michael. They seem to be feeding you up. And not before time, I would say. He was always frighteningly thin,' she remarked to the nurse who smiled pleasantly before departing about whatever a nurse's business was.

Michael was staring straight in front of him, eyes wide open, a little tic in his jaw.

Not given to censuring her own thoughts these days, Susan, in abstract moments, would try to imagine the physical damage allegedly caused to Michael's brain by the smoke. She might think of the inside of him being grey, charred, turning a new colour now, like the scar on her temple. He coughed drily as if in affirmation of her speculations. His lungs had been very badly affected and the doctor said his heart would have to work very hard to compensate for their reduced capacity, putting great strain on its arterial walls and chambers. And yet he never seemed especially breathless. 'Mother's well, though still no word from Father. For all that he used to put her through, she still misses him. Doesn't make sense, does it?'

She took off her black gloves and held Michael's hand, a dry white thing nestling in the warmth of her palms. Away in some other part of the ward a man yelled, once and sharply, and placatory female voices could be heard offering a simultaneous reply. 'Mother would have come today but she thinks you get upset when people visit you. Would you say that was true, Michael? Do you get upset when I come to see you?'

His eyes were fixed on the hearts-and-flowers chintz wallpaper on the long wall in front of them. Then he glanced towards the high window and made a rolling motion with his lips that not long ago Susan, in her imagination, might have taken to be a genuine response, an attempt at a smile perhaps. 'Are you upset now, Michael?'

He did not answer. He never answered. The two remained there in silence for the next ten minutes, Michael's only movement in that time being to scratch the stubble on his chin which seemed to be irritating him. Susan breathed deeply and looked at her watch. 'I must be going now,' she said, putting her gloves back on and going to the open door to beckon the nurse who jumped quickly from her seat at the far end of the lounge. She bustled in through the door.

'Have you enjoyed your wife's visit, Mr Crumly?' she asked, leaning her weight over him.

'Will you leave him here?' Susan asked.

'He seems happy enough, don't you think? Anyway, it'll be tea-time shortly, then I can sit him up to the table,' said the nurse.

Susan bent over him and hugged him, kissing his rough cheek.

And I did love you once after my own fashion . . . limbs among the tumbled sheets . . . your presence . . .

His hand suddenly shot up, grabbing Susan's wrist.

'Silly,' Susan said playfully. 'I have to go now.'

'Come along, Michael,' the nurse said, intervening to surround his thin wrist with her large hand. 'Let go now.'

He began breathing rapidly, making odd hiccuping noises in his throat.

Susan freed herself. 'I think it might be best if I went,' she said, stepping back a pace, rubbing her wrist which had become quite red beneath the glove.

'That might be wise,' the nurse said, still gripping Michael's hand, leaning heavily into him.

'Goodbye, Michael,' Susan said, offering a gloved wave. 'I'll call again soon. Next week. Yes?'

The nurse was struggling now, sweating a little, though smiling yet. 'Best be off,' she said. 'While the going's good.'

Susan composed herself before leaving the ward. Outside the front door of the home she paused to put on her red woolly beret. Then she walked away through the gardens where a new light rain was falling and the earth was wet and the grey skies were broken with white.

PAUL SAYER
THE COMFORTS OF MADNESS

Winner of the Whitbread Book of the Year Award

'A *tour de force* of the imagination'
The Times

'The unvoiced monologue of a 33-year-old catatonic patient in a mental hospital . . . Peter's moving dissertation bears witness to a world which denies all rights to the mentally ill . . . Lucidly and economically written, Paul Sayer's first novel is a remarkable achievement'
The Sunday Times

NIGEL WATTS
BILLY BAYSWATER

'A beautifully crafted imaginative expression of one very particular view of the world'
Judy Cooke in The Guardian

'This fine and careful novel about those who live on the margins of our society is an indictment of that society without saying a word against it. Billy suffers. His lack of resentment makes us condemn our culture of indifference'
Andrew Sinclair in The Times

sceptre

RICHARD WALKER
A CURIOUS CHILD

'Extraordinarily well-constructed, artful, daring and imaginative'
Timothy Mo

'Entirely admirable account of the decline and degeneration of a prosperous, "normal", middle-class English family. The prose is consistently exquisite'
The Times

JONATHAN COE
A TOUCH OF LOVE

'Witty and astringently intelligent'
Robert Nye in The Guardian

'A moving tale about an ageing postgraduate student of English at a university in Coventry . . . old friends and beloveds prove no bulwark against rising despair, especially when a necessary pee in the park bushes gets Robin charged with child molestation . . . all pessimistically magnetic stuff'
Valentine Cunningham in The Observer

sceptre